Advanced Praise for

"As a youth she knew she was different. The Golden Child, Enchanted, Gifted and Blessed were words rarely reserved for young black girls in the 1920's yet she was all of those things and more. This beautiful insightful girl would prove to be a renaissance woman in her time and lay down traditional patterns that would alter the lives of modern black women for generations to come. "

"This is beautiful!!! ... Love it! So glad that you are doing this."

Mrs. Kathleen Edmond

"...Engrossing, informative, and uniquely expressive...The Quiltmakers is a deeply spiritual tale that honors the synergy of Eastern and Western medicine as seen through the eyes of the African American community ; a true celebration of life, love, and Black female empowerment.

Dr. Jeremey Moore M.D.

"Love It! Very inspirational "

Dr. Cathy Franklin RN PhD

"It had me on an emotional roller coaster, in a good way. Congratulations to you and your sister. I cannot wait to see the response to this Phenomenal book!"

Dr. Serena Satcher M.D.

THE QUILTMAKERS

* * *

By

Dr. B.K. Edmond

And

Ms. Cassandra Edmond

Info@TheBEdmondProject.com
5320 Woodnote Lane Columbia MD 21044

Credits:
Illustrations by Zsa Zsa Lambert Hall and Nexxlevel RTR Solutions
Cover Design by Orlando The Designer

ISBN: 979-8-835089727

First Edition June 2022 by Amazon Publishing

Find Out More about B. Edmond by Taking a Picture of the QR code and clicking the link

The B. Edmond Project Website

Contents

✳ ✳ ✳

Foreword
by Dr. Michael Lindsay MD MPH

* * *

Maternal mortality is a tragedy for the newborn, the family, and the community. African American women are 3 times more likely than white women to die in childbirth in the United States. **The Quiltmakers** is a riveting short story about the important role a supportive and engaged community can play in reducing the risk of severe maternal morbidity and mortality.

The Quiltmakers is a must read. It is a story of professional success, family love, personal loss, and a resilient community. The story clearly articulates key factors related to black maternal mortality and offers a historical perspective of the important role played by granny midwives, and folk medicine, in decreasing adverse pregnancy outcomes. It also provides links to contemporary resources for prospective mothers and their families to become better educated about this important public health topic.

The protagonist of this story is an African American reproductive age anesthesiologist who practices in an urban medical center in Atlanta. She expertly manages a near miss maternal mortality and in the process of re-viewing the clinical case for quality improvement discovers that she resides in the state with the highest maternal mortality ratio in the United Sates. She is disturbed and intrigued by the disparity in black /white maternal mortality in her state and seeks to find reasons and solutions for the disparity.

Her quest for answers takes her back to her rural Georgia hometown to attend her younger sister's baby shower. During her interactions with elders and matriarchs of the community no one could remember a maternal death in their close-knit black community. She was surprised and sought to find the explanation for the discrepancy in black maternal mortality in this rural community compared to the rest of the state. She was ultimately able to uncover through events related to her younger sister's delivery and postpartum complication, the reasons for the low maternal mortality in her home community.

Michael Lindsay MD, MPH
Professor Gynecology Obstetrics
Emory University

The Quiltmakers

✳ ✳ ✳

This is dedicated to the mothers of the African American Community who unselfishly give life to our future while risking their own. It is for the sisters, daughters, cousins, aunts, wives, girlfriends and lovers who participate willingly in the beautiful creative revolutionary act of birth; thus, affirming daily each black child's value to this world.

On this day may the cries of mothers lost be heard and their parting whispers of love for their infants left behind unite to form a mighty wind.........Then SHOUT! .... That trembles the foundations of American Medicine and topples the walls of Healthcare Disparities like Jericho's into a fine dust.

"She saw a dust bearing bee sink into the sanctum of a bloom; the thousand sister-calyxes arch to meet the love embrace and the ecstatic shiver of the tree from root to tiniest branch creaming in every blossom and frothing with delight" Janie's description of a natural love <u>Chapter 2 Their Eyes Were Watching God </u>by Zora Neil Hurston

CHAPTER 1

✳ ✳ ✳

HER THUNDERSTORMS

omething's not quite right…

Dr. Altha Harkens looked at her patient's blood pressure on the monitor and felt tension growing in her chest. She was in the ninth hour of a twenty-four-hour shift on the labor and delivery floor. She was a junior attending—one of the few Black female anesthesiologists or "sleep doctors" as her mother affectionately called her—working at one of the premier medical centers in Atlanta, Georgia.

Anesthesia was one of the few fields where being a little obsessive compulsive was a good thing. Especially for her patients. Watching the blood pressure ticking slightly lower than she was comfortable with set her OCD into action. Altha wanted to see the vital signs perfect, but they weren't, so she acted. As a precaution, she gently placed another large-sized I.V. in her patient's arm. If things went bad, they would need to get large amounts of fluid into the patient in a short period of time. As soon as the line was in, she turned to the nurse.

"Can you call Dr. Smith back?"

The obstetrician had left the OR after he finished stitching the incision he made in the patient's uterus to get the baby out, and stapling her belly back together.

The nurse raised an eyebrow. "Dr. Smith? Everything okay?"

The nurse followed Altha's eyes to the monitor and then looked down at the patient and then finally landed her eyes on Altha's face. Altha had done enough C-sections with this experienced L&D nurse that Nurse Baskins could see on her face that everything was indeed not okay.

Altha shook her head. "He needs to come back and take a look down below. Something's not right." She voiced the feeling swimming around in her belly.

Nurse Baskin nodded and quickly walked over to the phone on the wall and made the call. The whole exchange was so subtle that everyone else in the room missed it.

Things had started off well. In fact, the whole day had been a good one so far, except for the argument she'd had with Dr. Hanson, a third year anesthesiology resident training under her guidance. He was a bit of a know-it-all who had provoked Altha to dig deep into her patience vault to deal with him.

At the beginning of her shift, she was running her morning checklist and asked him to make sure the emergency delivery operating room was set up and ready to go, including the videoscope. That was something Altha loved about working in this hospital. They had the most up-to-date, state-of-the-art equipment. This particular instrument made it easier to place a breathing tube when a patient had to be intubated for a C-section.

"The team that left this morning didn't have to use the room, so it should be cool. The videoscope should be there." Dr. Hanson kept his eyes on the chart he was updating, not even giving her the respect of looking at her when he talked to her.

Altha frowned. "Can you check it anyway? We can't just count on the fact that everything is there and set up."

Dr. Hanson bit his lip and let out a deep breath.

I know he didn't just roll his eyes at me.

Altha gave Dr. Hanson a look. For some reason, he needed to be reminded on a regular that she was the one in charge. He answered to her.

She shook her head and let it pass. Was he suffering a bad case of senioritis since he was mere months away from graduating from the training program? No, he just had a baseline bad attitude.

Other than that, the day had gone well. The baby deliveries for the day had been steady. There had been two scheduled cesarean sections performed in the operating room in the morning that went well.

This particular delivery had started out really well too. Altha had met the family earlier on the L&D floor when she put in the patient's epidural. The husband, Mr. Carlton Murphy, was a towering, thickly built 6'5" 300 pound, tan colored brother whose body could fill a door. Altha had smiled watching the father-to-be tenderly doting on and caring for his beautiful, brown-skinned wife as the contractions increased.

Although a beaming, thirty-seven-year-old woman having her first child, Mrs. Tasha Murphy was heavier than she needed to be and had been on medications to manage her blood pressure. Her lab work looked good though. And the baby looked great on the monitor too. The new mother-to-be had been in labor since late last night and was moving along well until the afternoon when things slowed down for her. She was comfortable, but her labor had stalled so the obstetrics team scheduled the C-section.

Not long after they wheeled Mrs. Murphy from the labor & delivery room 8 to the OR to perform the surgery, Altha explained everything to her patient. "You already have the epidural in place. Now we're going to just give a slighter stronger medicine and your numbness will go from the bottom of your chest to just above your knees." Altha used her hand to demonstrate where the numbness would be.

"From the top of your belly up, you'll feel normal. You'll be completely awake and able to talk and participate in the beauty of your child's birth." Altha patted the woman's shoulder reassuringly. The patient was one of those that came in with a complete birth plan. She was disappointed to be having a C-section rather than a normal vaginal delivery. But she remained cheerful. Altha could feel from her smile that she was one of those beautifully optimistic people who always saw the glass as half full.

"Sounds good, Dr. Harkens. I'm glad you're here. Thanks for taking care of me." They shared a smile. Altha could read between the lines. The smile on Mrs. Murphy's face said, *I'm glad a sistagirl is taking care of me.*

In the operating room, the excitement of the coming child filled the room with expectation. Tasha Murphy followed instructions like a champ. The delivery was smooth sailing.

Carlton Murphy was all smiles when he laid eyes on his brown, shining, infant girl. He left his wife's side and walked over to the incubator to watch as the pediatricians made sure his new addition to his family was in good health. The child was healthy and doing great.

"She's so beautiful." His voice was raw with pure emotion. "She has your chin!"

Tasha smiled and craned her neck to steal a peek at her daughter. Altha would never get tired of the emotions coursing through the room right after a delivery, whether C-section or vaginal. Her heart filled with joy for this couple that had waited so long for this little miracle.

The tender, intimate look the couple shared made Altha think of her own life. There was a little pang in her heart. She was proud to be a board certified anesthesiologist, but accomplishing this goal required a focus and discipline that drew her into an academic world that didn't leave much time for a social life. She had achieved her professional goals, but she wasn't married. But she was happy and content and had made her family proud. Having completed her training, she felt as if she was just lifting her head up and starting to refocus on what her life should be about.

When Altha finished her anesthesiology training in San Francisco, she chose to return to Atlanta, the city she fell in love with during her undergraduate days at Spelman College. More importantly, she was returning to the state of Georgia to be nearer to her family. Now instead of crossing the country to come home for infrequent visits, she only had to drive two hours down I-75, then onto Route 16 to get to the family homestead about forty minutes south of Macon in Dudley, Georgia.

Home was where her mother Annabelle lived and her father Jacob, who inspired and supported Altha, lay. Jacob "Sonny" Harkens passed away suddenly when she was in her third year of medical school. He was the first person to ever call her "doctor," a title he gave her when she graduated from high school. She had not been the first in the family to leave Dudley, but academically and professionally, she had flown the highest and was one of the first doctors of the grandchildren and great grandchildren of Big Poppa Willie Earl Harkens, the family patriarch.

"I'm a father. I have a beautiful baby girl." Carlton Murphy's voice brought Altha back to the room. Dr. Smith, a well-trained obstetrician, looked up at her from his end of the OR table. He spoke to one of the nurses.

"Have you started the oxytocin yet? Her uterus is a little boggy and is oozing a bit more blood than I'd like. The placenta is out. Let's get that uterus clamped down."

Altha nodded and opened the line with the fluid containing the normal post-delivery dose of oxytocin. Despite this, Mrs. Murphy's blood pressure was lower than normal. Altha started other medicines to keep it in a safe range.

The OR was still abuzz with excitement. The new mother was comfortable, and the new father was happy. The entire family was moved from the operating room and welcomed by a nurse into the surgical recovery room.

Jai McKinney, a first year anesthesiology resident also under Altha's tutelage, began reporting the operating room events to the receiving recovery room nurse. Altha noticed each time she tried to turn down the medicine supporting Mrs. Murphy's blood pressure, the blood pressure would drop. As her blood pressure was decreasing, her heart rate was increasing. Altha frowned at the monitor. That's when the voice in her head started whispering those dread-filled words, *Something's not quite right.*

Dr. Smith finally arrived in the recovery room. The five minutes it took for him to come felt like hours. "Dr. Harkens, what's happening?"

"I'm not able to decrease the meds supporting her blood pressure. And her heart rate is slowly increasing."

He nodded and moved to the end of the gurney Mrs. Murphy was lying on.

There in the last rays of sunlight, the new father fawned over his beautiful baby girl as she cooed and calmly rested under his watchful eyes. The image was sublime, tranquil in a way that only the wonder of a sleeping newborn infant perfectly formed by the Creator can inspire.

Tasha Murphy smiled at her husband and baby, but then her face contorted. She grabbed her belly. "I feel a cramp. It's as bad as the contractions." She grabbed the bedrails and let out a scream.

Altha looked at the clock, knowing her evening was about to take a 180-degree turn into a rapid paced, life or death scenario that she'd trained for over the years.

Dr. Smith opened Tasha's legs to check her. A river of blood came rushing out. He climbed on the gurney, holding pressure to her uterus.

Altha and Jai began rolling the new mother back towards the emergency use operating room. Altha sent out an emergency "All Call" to have any available on-call anesthesiologist come to the labor and delivery ward operating room to help.

A year out from her residency, she knew how to be a leader

when under fire and immediately calmed herself and began prioritizing. The team entered the room, then quickly lifted the mother onto the operating room table and began preparing to emergently sedate her.

Dr. McKinney began placing monitors on Mrs. Murphy, and Dr. Hanson came in the room with more anesthesia staff. They started life stabilizing fluids wide open, running into the large IV that Altha had the presence of mind to put in when she first became concerned about the blood pressure.

"Dr. Hanson, please set up the videoscope. We'll need to intubate her."

"I don't think we need it. We'll be able to intubate with the regular equipment."

Altha turned away to continue to draw up some high strength blood pressure medicine to use if the mother's system didn't tolerate the emergent medications used to put her to sleep.

As Altha finished preparing the medicine, she turned back to the patient. Dr Hanson still hadn't set up the airway videoscope.

"Dr. Hanson, please set up the videoscope." Her voice was much firmer. "We need to put her to sleep." Altha turned back to the monitor, looking at the blood pressure and heart rate, calculating exactly how much time they had before things got as bad as it looked like they might.

"Do we really need it? We should be able to get the breathing tube in easily." Dr. Hanson was trying her. Really trying her.

Altha turned to another one of the anesthesia staff. "Let's activate the Massive Transfusion Protocol." They needed the hospital blood bank to quickly deliver a large amount of the major parts in blood needed to help Mrs. Murphy stop bleeding.

A nurse responded that the emergency blood products were on the way. As Altha picked up the syringes filled with sedatives from the top of the anesthesia cart and turned to approach the operating room bed where Mrs. Murphy would have to fight for her life, she was amazed to see Hanson still had not set up the videoscope.

She stared at him. "Enough! You're not hearing me and you're distracting my energies from the patient. Leave the room! NOW!"

When she gave the command, the operating room that was buzzing with the urgent conversations of five surgeons, five anesthesia providers, three labor nurses, three surgical technicians and one anesthesia technician froze in silence.

Altha's next words to Dr. Hanson sliced through the air. "I don't know what's wrong with you, but your not hearing me is getting in the way of taking care of this patient. You're not the focus—the patient is."

Dr. Hanson still frozen, stiffened his back, eyed Altha with generational hate, then slowly marched out of the room.

Without missing a beat, she calmly pointed to Dr. McKinney. "Please get the videoscope and prepare to handle the airway."

Within seconds, Tasha Murphy was asleep and the doctors, nurses and technicians began to gel into a team. An arterial line to more closely monitor blood pressure was placed lightning fast and the new mother was transfused the blood products giving her the best chance at survival. Altha administered lifesaving medications to give the surgeons more time to find the source of the bleeding.

The tide of blood loss initially increased, but then thankfully began to slow. The rhythm of the resuscitation team was poetry in motion as the surgeons, nurses and anesthesia team began to flow working in unison. Actions were completed in quick response to the surgical team's needs and slowly, what was dread in the operating room began to transition to hope. The bleeding stopped and Mrs. Murphy stabilized.

She was not out of the woods and would have to go to the intensive care unit with the breathing tube still in place, but her lab work and vital signs suggested she should be okay. Of most importance, the surgeons did not have to remove her womb, the last-ditch effort for extreme bleeding after a delivery. The Murphy couple would be able to create more beautiful babies in the future.

Before the team left the operating room, underneath each

team member's mask, some stained with blood, there were solemn smiles of quiet confidence as they reflected on how quick their system was to recognize the post-operative bleeding and transition to getting the new mother on the operating room table. It had been a matter of minutes to get her asleep then opened and saved. The excellent surgical skills supported by anesthesia had allowed them to have a win. Every doctor enjoys a true save.

The team's good feelings were short lived. As they rolled the new mother with breathing tube still in place down to the intensive care unit and passed by the door of the surgery recovery, a bone-chilling, painful wail came from the new father. It felt like the wail shook the walls of the long hallway and spoke of Mr. Murphy's realization that he might become a widower on the same day he became a father.

As Altha passed the room, the mountainous man was fallen, lying on the floor in a fetal position, having been made small by his current circumstances. His painful wails were only cut short by his sobbing and repeating a refrain, "What am I going to do without you? What am I going to do without you?"

Altha wanted to stop to reassure him that all would be well. But she wasn't sure of that and was never one to give a family false hope. No one on the team had the answer for him as all eyes were now cast down and focused on moving the object of his love, his wife, to the intensive care unit.

After helping to drop off Mrs. Murphy in the ICU, Altha left her team to return to the operating room to help reset it, knowing that at any minute, another emergent case could arise. As she entered the operating room, now with no patient and the cadre of providers gone, the room felt different. Beeping alarms from the unattached ventilator and ringing alarms from the blood pressure cuff formed an eerie syncopated rhythm and were the only sounds in the room.

She scanned past the empty blood product bags lying in the corner and rested her eyes on the operating room table. The image that burned an impression into her was the amount of blood on the floor. It was still slowly dripping from the bed. It was only then that Altha, who had nerves of steel and an unearthly ability to focus during a crisis, experienced a whole body shudder.

Altha needed to catch her breath as the realization of the incredible amount of energy and focus she expended during the case took its toll on her body. As she looked down, she noticed for the first time her blood-soaked scrub pants legs that told a story of how physically close and mentally involved she had been in the case. She headed to the locker room, knowing she needed to shower and change into new scrubs to complete her shift.

In the locker room, before Altha could fully undress, she collapsed on a bench and exhaled, only to reflexively bend over and cover her mouth with both her hands to stifle her silent scream that transformed into raspy sobs as she cried, remembering the father's mournful wail.

What could she have done better? Were her efforts enough? Were their team's efforts enough to win that precious newborn a mother, or would their efforts fall short and leave a newborn, motherless child? Had it really taken less than an hour for Mr. Murphy to go from one of life's greatest gains to potentially one of life's greatest losses?

For a fleeting second, the thought of the pushback from having kicked Hanson out of the operating room entered Altha's mind. That almost never happened. She would have to take her time writing up the quality assurance report that was mandatory whenever a routine case needed intensive care unit aftercare.

Altha shook off the heavy weight of emotions threatening to take her spiraling down a black hole. She stood and stretched her mahogany brown, athletically sculpted arms to the sky. She turned to the mirror in the locker room to see her reflection. She was 5' 10" and slim, but even in the green doctor's scrubs, her thirty-year-old body showed hints of how fit and toned she was.

After she showered, she walked into the doctor's lounge, glad to find that no one else was there. The floor-to-ceiling windows gave her a perfect view of the Atlanta skyline. A storm chain passed across the city earlier in the day, washing the pollen out of the air. Altha took in a cleansing breath as she stood and gazed in awe at the orange, purple and pink colored clouds proclaiming a beautiful evening.

Her mother always told her there were silver linings in storm clouds, but it had taken years for her to understand that the most breathtakingly brilliant sunsets followed a good old-fashioned, Georgia thunderstorm.

She sighed. After the storm she had experienced taking care of Tasha Murphy, hopefully the rest of the evening would be as beautiful as the sunset.

CHAPTER 2

✳ ✳ ✳

SWIMMING WITH SHARKS

The next morning, having survived the rest of the call, Altha entered her apartment, went straight to her couch and curled up under her favorite quilt from home to take a nap. She had slept a little at the hospital, as the rest of the night was uneventful, but still could use a few more hours of sleep.

She preferred the couch to her bed at that moment. When she was emotionally stressed, her huge, king-sized bed seemed gargantuan and empty. After almost losing a patient, she wanted nothing more than to find safety and comfort curled up in the arms of a beautiful, kind-hearted man who loved her. But there wasn't one in her life. And she didn't need to be reminded of that in that big empty bed, all by herself. For this post-call sleep, her couch would have to do.

When she arose at noon, she set about the task of preparing her write up for the "C-section take back." She knew it was always best to get quality assurance paperwork for cases prepared close to the day of the event.

Whenever an unexpected event occurred in the hospital, a special write up for the in-house quality assurance team was done.

It included the patient's history, risk factors for the outcome and operating room course events. It closed with a summary of the staff physician's best guess at what caused the outcome and a list of actions that could be taken to improve patient care. The attending staff—Altha in this case—would present the case to the entire department to emphasize the teaching points. However, at times, the discussions could get testy and combative as different doctors debated their individual approaches to care.

Fortunately, at the University of California San Francisco, her medical school mentor, Dr. Allan Perkins, a white, soft-spoken anesthesiologist, trained her to "swim with sharks." For years, seasoned physicians trained their younger counterparts on how to survive in a hostile hospital work environment based on a hundred-year-old article entitled, "How to Swim with Sharks." The original article was meant to train sponge divers who regularly worked in shark infested waters, but it was perfectly appropriate for the hospital setting.

A bad outcome and her having to kick a resident out of the room would surely create enough blood in the water and drama to attract the sharks in the anesthesiology department.

While there were ten rules on swimming with sharks, three of them came to Altha's mind for her current situation. The first was, "Don't bleed—even if you are injured, don't show weakness as you might start a feeding frenzy. "As she mentally prepared for Monday, she promised herself not to display any weakness or uncertainty in front of her peers.

The next rule was crucial. "Counter any aggression towards you promptly. Sharks rarely attack a swimmer without warning. Usually there is a tentative exploratory aggressive action. It is important that the swimmer recognize this behavior as a prelude to an attack and takes prompt remedial action. The appropriate counter move is a sharp blow to the nose."

She was a relatively young staff member and knew someone or ones would be coming to her to gauge her ability to academically defend herself. She promised herself to be ready. The third rule for her to remember was, "Assume all unidentified fish are sharks." Word would get out on the department's grapevine about the case and her kicking the resident out of the operating room. Altha didn't know from which direction the colleague sharks would come, but she knew the game.

Altha was expecting to have to motivate herself to get the write-up completed, but after reading the first few articles on risks factors for post-delivery bleeding and possible death, she became engrossed. She lost track of time as she saw the headlines and articles on the high risk of death surrounding pregnancy for Black women. It seemed to affect all Black women, regardless of wealth or education.

Altha gasped in disbelief as she read of millionaire tennis sensation, Serena Williams', description of how she had to ask nurses repeatedly for assistance when she had a blood clot to her lungs following her delivery. She was in tears as she read of Black women—businesswomen, educators, lawyers and even Black physicians like herself who had excellent prenatal care, yet passed away during pregnancy.

As she focused on her patient's history, she was able to identify numerous risk factors that may have contributed to her problems including it being her first child, obesity, age greater than thirty-five, high blood pressure and prolonged labor. The risk factor that stood out the most was her being African American. That alone made her three times more likely to die surrounding childbirth than her white sisters in motherhood. The weight of the issue became near unbearable as Altha read the fact that, out of all states, Georgia had the highest incidence of death surrounding childbirth for African American women.

Altha set the last article down in disgust and began to digest what she had read. She walked into her kitchen to grab something to eat. She popped a pod in her Keurig and grabbed a prepackaged salad from the refrigerator. They had become a staple during her busy residency days and she had continued the habit since returning to Georgia. A wheat baguette finished the meal.

She brought her food and drink to the coffee table and sat down, still reeling from the information she had learned about her home state and maternal mortality.

Georgia was the heart of the south's economy and home to Atlanta—the new place to be for the film industry, Black entrepreneurs and African American affluency. Atlanta was the city of the phoenix, home to multiple historical Black colleges and even a Black medical school. In Georgia, state of the art healthcare was talked about as if it was available to all. In reality, Georgia was failing Black women at their most vulnerable time—during childbirth.

From her reading, there seemed not to be a single cause that could be addressed, but a group of problems whose combined outcome was an increase in the death of Black mothers surrounding childbirth. Numerous scientists, physicians and women's health providers were rising to the challenge, but they were still at the beginning stages. Researchers knew what was happening, but not exactly why.

Altha finished her salad and bread, and sipped her now not so hot coffee as she began to finish the summary on the presentation and write up. She had to decide whether listing the patient's race as a stand-alone risk factor would cause any pushback from her colleagues. She was one of ten women anesthesiologists and one of four Black anesthesiologists in the department of nearly eighty doctors and nurse anesthetists. She had to consider if mentioning race would lead the discussion in a direction that her colleagues couldn't handle.

Did she want to risk being labeled as a Black radical? Was mentioning race worth it? Maybe it would be best to stick to the general risk factors and not delve into the specifics on this patient. She finished the summary, saved the write-up and went out for a jog.

On Monday morning, it was back to work. Altha quietly leaned on the back wall of the elevator, heading up to the labor and delivery floor. She was joined by several people, two of which were African American women who reminded her of her aunts in Dublin, Georgia. That sweet feeling of familiarity faded as she couldn't help but overhear their conversation.

"She was healthy as a horse, just coming in to have her baby and now she's in the ICU, fighting for her life," the older one said.

The second one said, "We have to keep praying for her and Carlton."

The older woman nodded and added, "What if she doesn't make it? Who's going to help with the child? She did all her pre birthing visits and followed instructions. I don't understand how this could happen."

"I don't know, but someone must have messed up. I wouldn't be surprised if someone in this hospital gets sued."

Altha froze and her heart skipped a beat. She remembered her medical school ethics class where she was told she would be involved in some type of legal action every seven years she practiced. She had not been in a malpractice lawsuit, but she knew doctors who had, and the experience had changed their lives. Sometimes bad things happened to patients as a result of true malpractice—some sort of negligence or mistake on the doctor's part. Many times though, even if you did things exceeding the standard of care, you would have to defend your practice in front of a lawyer during the fact-finding part of a lawsuit at a grueling deposition. It could be financially costly some of the time, but was emotionally costly all the time.

Altha stepped off the elevator and turned towards her office. As she looked up, she was approached by Dr. Ryan Steel, a stiff-necked colleague she tolerated, but didn't have any relationship with, and Dr. Manuel Romero, another junior staff who seemed to be nice. Dr. Steel was a definite shark, and since Dr. Romero was swimming next to him, he was a shark by default.

Dr. Steel gave Altha a tight smile. "I heard there was some crazy action on the labor delivery deck over the weekend. Heard the patient ended up in ICU and is still on the ventilator."

Altha looked him in the eye professionally and gave a noncommittal, "Yes, it was an interesting case."

Dr. Steel went on to say, "Todd Hanson, my mentee, said there was some sort of disagreement between you and him and that you asked him to leave the operating room. He seemed concerned when he spoke to me."

Altha gave a noncommittal, "Hmmm." Her senses recognized the shark's nudge, and she didn't take the bait of engaging in a conversation on Dr. Steel's terms. "I'm open to discussion on it in the future, but I'm just getting into work and need to focus on my cases for today."

As Altha walked off, she told Dr. Steel to email her, and they could schedule a time to talk.

Dr. Steele's voice followed her down the hallway. "I'm on the Quality Assurance committee and looking forward to reviewing your write-up and possible presentation for the entire department."

Altha didn't turn around. "My report will be turned in today." She was thankful she had anticipated needing to "punch the shark in the nose" by preparing her highly detailed write-up the day before.

When she entered her office, she immediately got down on her knees and said a quick prayer of thanks. If people knew how much she prayed over the course of the day, they would be amazed. Prayer was a constant in her life, and she carried a mini Bible given to her by her father in her waist pouch daily. She had carried the well-worn Bible in her pocket each day of medical school and residency and continued the habit into her professional years.

Before she arose from her knees, she knew she would request to go on vacation early to travel down to Dublin for her sister's baby shower which was scheduled for the coming Saturday. Her spiritual state could not wait until Friday to leave as planned. She needed to go today.

Before noon, the department scheduler cleared her calendar for the rest of the week and her three-day weekend vacation turned into a seven-day vacation in Dublin. This would be her longest time down home since she returned to Georgia.

CHAPTER 3

✳ ✳ ✳

HIS THUNDERSTORMS

Brandon Johnson's pulse was racing a mile a minute. Sweat poured from his forehead. His breathing quickened as he struggled to awaken and overcome a torment he'd experienced almost daily for the past two years. In the panic of his semiconscious state, he knew this morning would be no different as he tried to escape his recurring nightmares. The only question was which of the two major losses in his life he would have to endure.

Within seconds, the familiar city of Eldoret in the Rift Valley of Kenya crystallized in his dream. He knew today he would relive the horrors of his second major loss in life—his wife, Neema. Although he continued to valiantly fight to quickly pass through the halls of his thoughts, he knew he would awaken to his own cries and a painful loneliness in the end.

Brandon's thoughts traveled back two years and pain gripped his heart.

He had taken Neema, his pregnant wife, to her thirty-six week check-up at the Moi Teaching Hospital the day before a planned trip. In three weeks, he would be a dad again. It would be a boy to join his sister, Jameli. Brandon had committed to a five-day business conference and training session in the city of Namanga, near the Tanzanian border. With a day for travel each way, he would only be gone a week. With the birth of Jameli having gone without problems and plenty of friends who were there to help Neema as needed, he left knowing he would make the thirty-seven week check.

Neema called him the first day of the conference, when he just arrived. "This pregnancy is disturbing more than Jameli's. My hands and face are swelling and also my feet. It's funny the things a baby will do to a woman."

"Please make sure you rest and put your feet up. And drink lots of water."

When he talked to her two days later, she had new symptoms. "Now my stomach is upset and the right upper part of my belly hurts. I thought I was finished with all the stomach problems of the first trimester."

"Should you go to the doctor?"

"No, it's nothing. Waithera said that since I'm having a boy, I'm having different symptoms from my first pregnancy. Boy pregnancies do all sorts of strange things to a woman."

"Okay, if she says so." Waithera had four sons and a daughter, so certainly she knew what she was talking about.

On the last day of the conference, she called complaining that she could hardly sew the clothes for the baby and work on the crafts for his nursery. "My eyelids are even swollen. I'll have to tell this baby something when he comes out."

They laughed together about all the trouble this baby boy was causing his mother, but Brandon had a nagging feeling in the pit of his stomach.

The day Brandon was supposed to come home from the conference, Neema called, not sounding like herself. "I think maybe I should go to the hospital." He could tell it was difficult for her to get a whole sentence out with stopping to catch a breath. "My chest is hurting. This doesn't feel normal. I think something may be wrong. Please hurry and come take me to the hospital."

"Neema, you can't wait for me. I'll call Janet and have her come get you to take you."

Brandon called Janet, packed quickly, and caught the next available public transport bus back home.

An hour into the ride, Janet called him, slightly hysterical. "When I got here, Neema was unconscious on the ground. She was shaking like she was having a seizure. We're on our way to the hospital."

Brandon's heart rose into his throat. "Please help Neema! And please call me with updates." He prayed the entire way home to Eldoret.

He didn't hear another word from Janet until he reached Eldoret and hoped that meant everything was okay. But when he arrived at the hospital, one look at Janet's face let him know that everything wasn't okay. That his entire world had just changed. Janet's eyes were bloodshot from crying and she was wringing her hands. He found out they had already taken his wife and unborn baby to the morgue.

The next days, weeks, and months were all a blur. Instead of bringing his wife and new baby home, he went home alone and empty. Trying to explain what had happened to his six-year-old daughter was heartbreaking. She couldn't understand why her mother had gone to heaven instead of coming home to her. Didn't Mummy want to let her play with her new little brother? Jameli's questions and confusion drove Brandon into deep despair.

He and Jameli clung to each other, both devastated by the losses. Jameli, the once talkative light of the room had become quiet and withdrawn. A month after the funeral, Brandon decided they needed a "time out" back in America and he contacted his aunt, Lilly Baker, his mother's sister and his last living relative. He and Jameli headed to Dublin, Georgia.

Thinking he could leave tragedy behind in Kenya, he returned to America after a ten-year absence only to find tragedy awaiting him each morning in the form of the recurring nightmares.

Brandon opened his tear-filled eyes and immediately began to pray until his pulse went down and he could catch his breath. He moved onto his knees and began counting his blessings and asked God for the strength to help his injured spirit make it through the day.

The irony of it all was that tragic losses were what drove him to Kenya in the first place. He had finished his undergraduate degree at Morehouse and had a life full of promise ahead of him. He was headed to Wharton School of Business to get his MBA before starting a career as a business executive.

But his life was upended when his mother and father were killed in a tragic automobile accident. During that horrible summer, through prayer and while grieving, he realized he wanted to change his professional track. While he knew money and finance were his gift, he also knew he wanted to have more of a lasting impact on the world. He joined the Peace Corps, and left the next year for work in Kenya where he was assigned as an English teacher. He also worked to help with community small business development.

His first year traveling and working in Kenya was dynamic and eye opening. He loved the culture and the heart of the people. The people lived in community in a way he hadn't experienced in America. The beauty of the place and the people brought some healing to his grief-filled heart.

He had finished his assignment and was making plans to leave when he met Neema. Neema was a science teacher at the distinguished Moi Girls High School and one of the best people he had ever known. Through the help of his in-country benefactors, the Rono family, he deftly navigated the steps of the traditional marriage. Her dowry was five quality cows and two sheep. His aunt, Lilly Baker, represented his family during the ceremony and participated in the family bonding act of drinking one cup of cow's milk with Neema's elders.

Jameli came two years later. Brandon picked up a master's in Business at Moi University. As Brandon began expanding his work with cooperatives, he attracted international recognition. Some of his women's small business proteges traveled to the United Nations and the U. S Senate to present their examples of how small businesswomen's cooperatives increased women's opportunities in their communities.

For a time, Brandon's life was perfect and his new family, new country and the warm people softened his past losses. His heart almost burst from his chest when he and Neema found out they were pregnant with a boy. That would make his family complete. His career was going well and he was making an impact in the lives of businesswomen in his community. His family was thriving. How could life get better?

He should have asked how it could get worse. Much worse. There were days he couldn't even get out of bed, except that Jameli needed to be bathed and fed. They both lay around the house, mourning in silence.

One day, Brandon decided they'd had enough grief. He made up his mind that they needed a change. A "time out" from their mourning. He made one phone call that solved everything. Aunt Lilly was happy to welcome them into her home. And so "home" to Dublin they went.

   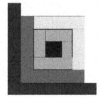

CHAPTER 4

✳ ✳ ✳

A MOTHER INDEED

Traveling home on I-75 South, Altha could feel herself relaxing. Her tension seemed to ease as she passed Stockbridge through Henry County. She could feel her breathing steady when she dropped below Macon. She passed the exit for Danville, knowing her destination was thirty more miles south. She would turn off Route 16, then head across the railroad tracks between two cotton fields, past Byrdhill Baptist church, that had been home to her family for ages. She would turn left onto Wayne's Road and drive past Rooks Cemetery, the family burial plot, before reaching the homestead.

Altha thought of her father as she drove. When Jacob "Sonny" Harkens passed away at the age of fifty-two in his sleep, those were trying times. He was a beautiful man, who loved his wife and family. He was a great role model and Altha's hero. His proudest day was her graduation from college. He realized he had spoken her destiny of becoming a doctor. Although her heart ached to even think about the loss the family endured, she found comfort in him knowing his oldest daughter was on a good track. At the time of his passing, his oldest son had chosen the Marines and the two other boys and the youngest girl were on track to go to college too. Sonny Harkens had done a father's job well.

As she neared the turn onto Wayne's Road, she recognized the driver of a blue, Ford 150 truck as it slowed. Aunt Flossie rolled down her window with a big "welcome home" smile as she waved.

"Hello, my little quiltmaker." That was Aunt Flossie's term of endearment for her. "I'm just leaving your mother's house. She told me you were on your way. When will I see you?"

Altha gave her a warm smile, feeling the joy of being home and being loved. "I promise to come see you before I leave. There's no way I can come to Dublin and not spend time with the master seamstress." They waved goodbye and parted ways.

Altha's joy grew when she rolled to a stop in front of the family home. There were seven other cars parked out front, as expected.

Over the years, the home had undergone numerous renovations, and the inside was modern. The grounds spoke of a centuries old homestead. There were two towering pecan trees on the back of the lot. On the front of the house, there were multiple, aged azalea bushes that were six feet tall and of all colors—white, red, pink, and purple. On the left side of the lot was a sweet gum tree that had to be at least 200 years old. It shaded part of the home. Also under its shade was an inviting handmade picnic table made by her father, Sonny Harkens, himself.

The fresh, country air was filled with the scents of a twelve-tree, pear orchard that was immediately behind the house between the pecan trees. In the two flower beds closest to the home, there were two bottle trees, made by putting blue and yellow colored bottles upside down on the tree limbs. The sun's rays passed through the bottles and painted the flower beds in blue and yellow rays.

The land had been in the family since Reconstruction after the Civil War and it was still unclear exactly how the patriarch, Big Papa Willie Harkens, was able to get it. Their home was nestled on a tract of land that belonged to her grandfather, Buddy Harkens, and then to her father, Sonny Harkens. It was currently not farmed, but there were still a couple of animals her mother took care of. The Harkens' home held good memories and was always filled with high energy.

Altha's brothers were spread across America. Altha was the oldest at thirty. Justin was a close second at twenty-nine years old, and lived in California serving as a Marine Sergeant. Next was Marcus who was twenty-seven years old and lived in Chicago where he worked in IT. Bay Joe was the youngest boy at twenty-six and lived in New York and worked on Wall Street. Everyone thought he would be the last, hence the name Bay Joe, short for Baby Joe. Bringing up the rear was the surprise baby, Teena or Tee, who was twenty-four years old.

Altha cringed a little bit when she thought of Tee. Early on, they were quite close since Altha, as the oldest girl, helped her mother raise her siblings. But Tee's problems started around the age of fifteen. Altha was away in college and began getting reports of Tee being difficult and rebellious. Tee made it through community college with decent grades, even though she was much smarter than her performance showed. After passing through those difficult years, she went on to Georgia Southern to finish her bachelors and get her teacher's certification. After college, she settled locally and was a well-loved preschool teacher in the community.

Where Altha was a tall, slim, studious introvert who tended to test her surroundings, Tee was the exact opposite who dove into life without a care. When looking at their faces, you could tell the two were sisters, but Tee was three inches shorter and by the age of thirteen, had filled out in a way that made men's heads turn and made even Altha envious.

Tee was a knockout, and eventually caught the eye of James Weldon. James was a former high school football star and starter on Georgia Southern's football team, who was now in local law enforcement. The two made a solid couple and James was tough enough to deal with Tee, who rarely held her tongue. No one was sure if Tee caught James or vice versa, but the end result was the coming first grandbaby for Anabelle and Sonny Harkens.

With Tee's Baby shower on Saturday, the women inside were sure to be hard at work, making sure her birthing quilt was at least halfway done. Quilting skills were a throwback tradition that were valued in the community and church.

As a child, Altha had been taught by Aunt Flossie how to expertly place and throw quality stitches. Aunt Flossie's whispered encouragement and patient guidance had made the young Altha a solid seamstress by the age of fourteen. Many began calling her "the Little Quiltmaker" in middle school. At the age of fifteen, Altha fell in love with science and stopped quilting. Since leaving home at eighteen for college, she hadn't been to a quilt sitting.

Passing the bottle trees and climbing up onto the front porch, Altha paused to steel herself and took a deep breath before entering. As soon as she crossed the threshold, Tee started in.

"Watch out, y'all. Here comes the city slicker." Tee, at nearly nine months pregnant sported a head-turning, silver teal blond, short trimmed hairdo and green contacts for the day.

Altha didn't have time to give her irritated response before her mother swooped in. "Altha, you're home." She gave her a long hug and planted a big kiss on her cheek. "I've missed you so much."

She turned to Tee. "Stop bothering your sister. How you gon' greet her like that when she first walks in the door? We're happy to see her, aren't we?" Annabelle Harkens said it like a warning. She was constantly keeping the peace between them, somehow accepting the fact that her two girls mixed like oil and water.

Altha's mother led her back to the room where the women were gathered quilting. She sat her down in a chair. "I know it's been a long time, but your hands will remember exactly what to do." She returned to the kitchen, seemingly happy she had delayed the battle between her daughters that would surely come.

At each stage in her life, Altha set the highest personal standards. In her discipline and in her studies, she was diligent. She made sure to surround herself with people who were trying to do good things and change the world. In her religious life, she prided herself on trying to keep the Ten Commandments and work for forces of light in the world and not darkness. But for all her awards and accolades, for all the academic hills she climbed, for all the people she unselfishly helped in her life, nothing could replace the relationship lost with her younger sister.

She reminded herself of the lesson she learned from her sister. Sometimes a good response is not good enough, and there are situations that must be handled perfectly the first time or repercussions can affect lifetimes.

Altha shook her head to ward off the thoughts of that time years ago when she and Tee's relationship fell apart. She didn't want to focus on it right now. She wanted to enjoy being home and enjoy being in the fellowship of the quilting circle. She could deal with her and Tee's demons later.

For now, she focused on the six women, expertly tailoring their cloth squares onto an almost half-finished quilt. She greeted the women, but had to stop at a new face—that of an eight-year-old girl who was sitting next to Mrs. Baker. The girl had arrestingly beautiful, smooth, black skin and the whitest of smiles. She was a stunning young beauty.

Altha moved to the seat next to her and introduced herself. "Hello, my name is Altha. What's yours?"

A sweet smile exploded across the young girl's face. "I'm Jameli."

"Nice to meet you, Jameli. How did you find yourself in our quilting circle?"

Jameli pointed to Mrs. Baker on the other side of her. "This is my aunt. But a great aunt. Like a grandmother. Or something like that."

Altha had to smile. She was sure someone had tried to explain it to the young girl, but it didn't quite make sense to her. Lilly Baker was one of her mother's oldest friends.

"Are you here for a visit or do you live in Dublin?"

"I am here for a time out." It was then that Altha could pick up an accent and she wondered where this little Black beauty was from.

Altha frowned. The response was peculiar, but it didn't seem like an appropriate conversation for the quilting circle. She decided to let it pass and leaned into the older women's conversation about church, children and stitching techniques.

Altha reached out for a square patch and a needle and thread. Slowly but surely, her hands began to remember the throws she was taught long ago by Aunt Flossie. She began with the Quilters knot one of the easiest and within minutes she was Stitching in the Dip, a more challenging maneuver. Altha's eyes were drawn to Jameli whose dark hands moved across the cloth and handled the thread like a master. Altha whispered to her, "You have beautiful hand movements that remind me of some really smart doctors I know. I bet you could be a surgeon one day."

The child smiled at the compliment and covered her pretty teeth with her hands.

Altha allowed herself to be swallowed up in the familiarity of home and the gentle banter of the women for a while, her hands fully remembering that they were quilting experts. She felt more relaxed than she had in a long time and found herself letting out deep breaths every once in a while.

After about thirty minutes of quilting and chatting, Altha felt her mother enter the room. Annabelle Harkens watched her quilt for a while with a proud smile on her face. The she took her by the hand and led her toward the front porch. They silently walked out past a scowling Tee who was still looking for a fight.

Once outside on the porch, Annabelle gave a sigh, grasped Altha's hand and pulled her daughter close to her side. She placed her arm around the hip of her oldest child and together they walked down the stairs. It was a position her mother used when she wanted to have a heart-to-heart talk with one of her children.

Her mother's pace was slow and thoughtful. She finally gave words to what was on her mind. "Altha, the baby shower is on Saturday, and you're here on Monday. Before you could get into the house, you were ready to fight with Tee. Something's going on. Do I need to get my posse and come up to the hospital?"

Altha laughed. Her mother could always read what was going on inside her. "No, Mama. You don't need to bring a posse up to the hospital.

Annabelle continued, "Remember what I told you."

The two repeated together in unison the advice Annabelle first gave Altha when she went away to college. "A crazy doctor ain't never helped nobody." The two smiled at Annabelle's special way of reminding Altha to take care of her health physically, spiritually and mentally.

As they strolled towards the side of the house approaching the fruit orchard, the emotional dam broke and Altha shared the events of her past three days. She shared her frustration at having to kick a resident out of the operating room just so she could save the new mother's life. She told of the screams of the new mother's husband and how it affected her to her core. She talked about how she searched the medical literature only to find out that Black women in America were dying at a rate three times higher than the average during birth, and that Georgia had the worst death rates. Her exasperation was palpable when she mentioned the potential lawsuit and the "sharks" at work she had to deal with regularly.

Her mother listened patiently, letting Altha vent. She finally spoke, "That all sounds really difficult." She cupped Altha's cheeks. "You've grown into such a strong, beautiful woman. I'm glad you came home for some rest and restoration, but I know when you get back, you'll handle everything with the intelligence and brilliance you always do. Things will be just fine."

Altha smiled. Her mother's confidence in her reminded her that she would indeed handle the situation well. She was glad she was home. Her mother's faith in her was just the boost she needed. If her father was there, he would have responded with the same faith and confidence in her abilities.

"You want to go see Mrs. Evelynn in the morning? You know I don't always have all the answers for you, but she always seems to."

As she had climbed the ranks of education, Altha knew her parents and now her mother didn't feel like they had the expertise to give her advice. Her mother often guided her to her godmother, Mrs. Evelynn. Mrs. Evelynn had a special way of viewing problems and guiding discussions to wise outcomes.

"Yeah, Mrs. Evelynn always knows what to do. She's helped us so much over the years."

Her mother gave her a weary smile and nodded. They walked to the pear orchard together, remembering their biggest issue they'd had to take to Mrs. Evelynn many years ago. That's when they had found out exactly what was wrong with Tee.

   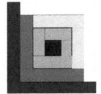

CHAPTER 5

✳ ✳ ✳

Sister To Sister

When Altha wanted to punish herself, she reminisced back to fall of her sophomore year in college when she received a disturbing call from Tee while studying for an organic chemistry midterm. Tee was fifteen and a sophomore in high school, and honestly, was way smarter than Altha. But Tee had begun spending time with the wrong crowd and began skipping classes and track practices. Altha's mother confided to her that there was distance growing between Tee and her. Even her father had not been able to break through to her. Tee was barely on speaking terms with anyone in the house.

After a freshman high school year that was outstanding, Tee's grades were falling and she was drinking and occasionally smoking. This was against the teachings in the home. Sonny Harkens was a no-nonsense father with his sons, but with his daughters, he was tender. He valued and protected them with his life, but found it difficult to chastise them. He left it to Annabelle to fill in for his weak spot when it came to disciplining his daughters. The parents had been trying everything, but could not solve what was going on with their once extroverted youngest child.

While Altha was studying for her organic chemistry midterms, Tee called her. Altha recognized immediately that she had been drinking because her slurred speech was hard to follow. Altha had little time to commit to such foolishness and scolded her for drinking, reminding Tee that their father would have a fit.

Tee just kept saying, "You just don't know…you don't know what pressures I have to deal with."

"Tee, you're beautiful, intelligent and talented with a bright future."

"Beauty has its costs."

Altha could hear something in her baby sister's voice that screamed for her to drop her studying and pay close attention to what was going on with her.

Tee continued, "We've been lied to. Love isn't always kind and gentle. Love destroys lives and futures. What is love anyway?"

"What are you talking about? Is this why you're making bad decisions and failing school? Some boy you think you're in love with?"

Tee let out a deep, tired breath. "Like I said, you don't understand."

"Then help me understand, Tee."

"I don't even trust my own judgment anymore. What am I doing with my life?"

"You know how important school is. Don't you want to follow in my footsteps? You could go to Spelman, just like me. You're smarter than me. You could get a full scholarship. You're so intelligent in science, you could—"

"F$%#* science! You hear me? F$%@* science!" Tee started screaming and crying into the phone.

Altha started speaking soothing words into the phone while motioning to her roommate to let her borrow her cell phone. She called her mother and told her what was going on. Their mother went straight to pick up Tee, who was at a local park that was frequented by the high school drinking and smoking crowd. Once her mother, Annabelle, was there with Tee, Altha got off the phone and went back to the Herculean task of pulling an all-nighter to make a strong grade in organic chemistry.

Two days later, Altha was dozing in a mandatory school assembly in Sisters' Chapel at Spelman College. The guest speaker, an alumnus and expert in women's health, said something that penetrated Altha's sleepy haze. Dr. Dazon said, "They don't trust their own judgement."

Altha awoke with a start and opened her eyes to see a slide on the lecture screen that listed the symptoms of women who had been sexually abused. Altha's heart sank as she read, "depression, loss of interest in school, skipping classes and dramatic change in grades, substance use and abuse." When she read the phrase, "A victim loses trust in their sense of judgement," she was up out of her seat, moving towards the aisle, phone in hand, dialing her mother.

There on the steps of Spelman's historic Sister's Chapel, while the rest of the campus was learning how to identify college sisters who needed help, Altha was making a diagnosis on her younger sister.

Annabelle Harkens listened closely to Altha, then got off the phone, went straight to school to pick up Tee and take her to her gynecologist. After the doctor visit, Altha's mother called her weeping. Tee had admitted to being sexually abused. She was tight-lipped about what had happened. There were no physical injuries and Tee was still technically a virgin, but they knew that most of the injuries from sexual abuse were emotional and spiritual, not physical.

That weekend, Altha went home to Dublin. Her mother had reached out to Mrs. Evelynn for advice and the three Harkens women quietly made their way over to her home for a meeting. Mrs. Evelynn had invited her daughter Kathleen, a lawyer practicing in Savannah. She and Tee went into a separate room to talk.

When the meeting with Kathleen finished, the women gathered. Kathleen's voice was solemn as she looked at Tee with gentle eyes. "Something did happen to Tee, but she's chosen not to share. She's afraid that her father and brothers will take action and that things could turn out badly. She's afraid her father and brothers could end up in jail and the man badly hurt or even dead."

Annabelle and Altha looked at each other. Tee was right. The Harkens men would kill for the Harkens women—especially Tee.

The lawyer continued, "For now, the best thing you can do is offer her love and support, emotionally and spiritually. I recommend a therapist."

The three other women gathered nodded in agreement they would hold the secret close, but Altha wasn't satisfied with this outcome. She agreed that her father and brothers would probably kill the perpetrator and may end up in jail, but there had to be another solution.

Altha immediately began mentally creating a list of men Tee was exposed to. She initially suspected Tee's track and field coach. But she went into research mode. She contacted several women she had graduated high school with and asked if there had been any teacher that made them uncomfortable. Several phone calls later, she was in shock.

Mr. Simpkins, her own mentor and science teacher—the man who had encouraged and supported her pursuit of a career in science and had even written her recommendation letter for her application to Spelman—his name came up six different times, from six different women.

She thought back to the drunken call from Tee. "F$%#* Science!" Was that Tee's identification of the perpetrator? Was Mr. Simpkins the one who had touched Tee?

Altha rallied the six girls, and together, they filed an official complaint against Mr. Simpkins. He was investigated and dismissed from the school. Altha's mother said Tee cried for hours when she found out. Altha and Annabelle Harkens were fully convinced he had touched Tee.

Like the nurturing mother she was, Annabelle patiently

supported and helped to restore Tee. Tee changed schools, re-started on the right track and reconditioned her spirit.

Altha never told Tee what she had done to make sure Mr. Simpkins was investigated and dismissed. Over the years, she wondered if she should have. Would that have healed the relationship between her and her little sister that she had once valued and treasured?

   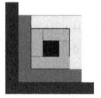

CHAPTER 6

✳ ✳ ✳

The Mystery Of The Safety Zone

The next morning, Altha arose early and placed a call to the Intensive Care Unit. She breathed a sigh of relief when she heard Mrs. Tasha Murphy had her breathing tube out and was doing well. The good news gave her energy to help with some chores. By 9 am, she and her mother were headed over to visit Mrs. Evelynn, now a seventy-year-old widow and grandmother.

As they exited the car, Mrs. Evelynn's wide body and deep bosom were dancing with excitement as she smiled and opened her beckoning arms to Altha. While hugging her, the first words out of Mrs. Evelynn's mouth, in her deep alto booming voice were, "Baby, you don't look right. Are you going crazy?"

Altha rolled her eyes and looked at her mother, who looked down at the driveway with a mischievous smile, feigning shame. Altha smiled and said, "No, I'm just pissed," as she continued to cut her eyes at her mother.

Mrs. Evelynn let out a loud laugh and guided them up the porch steps and into her aging house. "Come on in and tell me all about it. I'm sure we can figure out how to fix whatever…or whoever it is that's bothering you. I'm sure your Mama already told you we can put a posse together and bust up in that hospital if we need to."

The older women laughed together as Altha shook her head. "That won't be necessary, Mrs. Evelynn. I'm sure we can figure out something better than that."

Mrs. Evelynn had cooked a spread as if the whole Harkens family was coming to breakfast and not just Altha and Annabelle. As the women blessed the food and began to eat, Altha shared her recent experiences with Mrs. Evelynn. She discussed the whole scene in the detail while Mrs. Evelynn listened intently. When she mentioned that during pregnancy, Black women died at a three times higher rate, Mrs. Evelynn shook her head and said, "My, my, my…"

"And the state of Georgia has the highest death rate for Black women during birth in the whole country."

"Lord Jesus!" Mrs. Evelynn cried out.

Altha thought for a second and decided to find out about the experiences of the two older women. "How have you felt when you lost a friend, or relative, or someone you know during childbirth?" With the statistics being what they were, they both had surely lost several women within their sphere.

Mrs. Evelynn sat and thought for a second. "I haven't lost anyone during childbirth."

Altha frowned. "Hold on. You've been here all your life and you don't know a woman who died during childbirth?"

"Nope." Mrs. Evelynn shrugged.

Altha turned to her mother. "What about you?"

Her mother thought for a second. "I don't know anyone either. I've heard about it in Atlanta and Savannah, but not around here."

"How is that possible?" Altha was about to grill them further, but held her tongue and reminded herself she was with lay people in the country who just might not be aware of health issues. She made a mental note to look into it more when she got home to her computer.

✳ ✳ ✳

Later that evening, as Altha stared at the computer screen, she was intrigued. The Georgia public health registry on maternal deaths had a map of Georgia that was all red, or near red, except in the part of the county where she lived. When she dove deeper into the data, and separated the numbers out by race, the pattern held true. Mrs. Evelynn and her mother might be right. The statistics agreed with them.

It seemed they lived in a medical safety zone where there had not been a reported death of an African American woman during childbirth in many years. She wasn't expecting a medical mystery when she came home. But the fact the Dublin, Georgia was a safety zone when it came to maternal mortality was a mystery indeed.

"Game on…" she whispered to herself, accepting the challenge of solving the mystery as her mind shifted into analytical mode.

That evening, more women came by the home to add their unique pieces to Tee's quilt. She was surprised to see Jeanette Ross, Tee's high school archrival, and her mother casually enter their home, cloth in hand, to join in. When away in college and medical school, Altha would get reports of the epic battles—verbal and occasionally physical—between Tee and Jeanette. She wondered why it seemed Tee got along with everyone except her.

Joining a group of seven women, Jameli came with Mrs. Baker and sat next to Altha. They were halfway through the session when Altha posed her question to the group. "Do any of you know of someone around here who died during or surrounding childbirth?"

They all sat quiet for a moment thinking. Everyone said no, except Mrs. Baker, who asked, "Does the person have to be from around Dublin?"

"Yes, anyone around here," Altha clarified.

Mrs. Baker shook her head and added her "No" to the rest of the women's.

Altha then asked, "Why do you think Black pregnant women do better around here and don't have as many problems during birth as women in other parts of the state?"

Jeanette's mother said, "Slavery…they bred us that way."

Mrs. Jeffries shook her head. "We're protected by special haints and spirits."

Mrs. McKay declared, "It's the spring water and the ring tradition."

Altha jotted the suggestions down, remembering the local tradition of how men bring fresh spring water to the expectant mothers on the first day of each month during the pregnancy. She had almost forgotten about the men's tradition of giving a special birthing ring to be worn by the mother throughout the pregnancy.

She completed her notes, confident she had a solid list to begin her investigation.

This mystery doesn't have a chance.

When the session finished, Altha held Jameli's hand as she walked down the front stairs of her home. A car approached and Jameli pointed and shouted, "Daddy!" with glee. As the car stopped, a tall, brown-skinned man built like a wide receiver exited. He had a full, groomed beard with well-edged sideburns. His hair was in neat, curly dreads and his face sported classic Malcom X glasses. His smile was stunning and he had perfect teeth.

He walked to the bottom of the steps to meet them. "Is this the lady doctor my daughter was up all night talking about?" His voice was a rich, deep baritone. And it sounded strangely familiar.

Altha extended her hand. "Dr. Altha Harkens. Pleasure to meet you."

The gentle giant extended a warm soft hand and his brilliant smile shone even brighter as he said, "I am the Art…"

The phrase triggered something from deep in Altha's memory, and a reflexive verbal response leapt out of her. She didn't miss a beat and finished the stranger's sentence, "Aficionado!"

   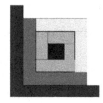

CHAPTER 7

✳ ✳ ✳

ART 101

B randon drew in a sharp breath, unable to believe the beauty that was standing before him. All these years later, and she was still as beautiful as when he first laid eyes on her. In fact, she was more beautiful.

Their paths crossed in an Art Appreciation class held at Spelman College during the Spring of 2007. The class was mandatory for students at the all-men institution, Morehouse College, and the all-women institution, Spelman College, but the class could be taken on either campus. The brash Morehouse senior, Brandon Johnson, was taking the course as one of his last requirements before graduation.

Brandon had planned his schedule perfectly. He was ending his years at Morehouse with one of his classes on Spelman's campus in the springtime. There was no hotter, more stimulating environment for an intelligent, African American brother who was into sisters than "on the yard." Over the course of an hour, hundreds of the most intelligent, beautiful, college-educated sisters convened by the manicured grounds surrounding Spelman's Manley Student Center. Brandon and his friend, Dexter, had sense enough to enroll in the Art Appreciation Class early and now their strategic planning was paying off.

Dr. Pierre-Louis read her vision statement from her syllabus, "Each of you will learn art, and the language of art, in hopes that as you advance in your respective careers, you will improve on your ability to see interpret and communicate your unique, God-given perception of this world. Your vision will sharpen as you grow to value the various mediums for expressing life, its experiences and its beauty. Art is not taught in a classroom, but must be experienced where the art is."

While 70% of the grade was dependent on classroom participation, 30% of the grade was dependent on a group project that required venturing to a variety of underground art exhibits throughout the city. In addition, there was a mandatory class fieldtrip to visit the Atlanta High Museum of Art, the flagship for the Atlanta art scene.

The Art Appreciation class was legendary, and Brandon knew he needed to make an A on the group project. He needed to put together a stellar team to do so. When Brandon entered Dr. Pierre-Louise's class, he scouted out the other students and saw one sister that piqued his interest. She was hard to miss at 5' 10" with a slim athletic build. She looked like she should be running the 200-meter on a track team, and didn't walk as much as glide through the crowd of students to get to her seat. Her smile flashed a set of perfect teeth, yet her most striking feature was her skin tone.

If he had to describe it to his mother, who appreciated descriptions of artistic masterpieces, he would call it deep, velvet black with points of textured silk that from an angle, when the light hit it just right, reflected the myriad of rainbow colors that black usually absorbs. Her skin dripped with youthfulness and had no blemishes, yet she carried herself as if she didn't know her own beauty. There was a confidence in her walk that didn't come from her looks, but from somewhere deeper in her character. More men would have noticed her, but for the thick, librarian glasses she wore that screamed, "Back up, brother. I'm into my books."

Brandon could easily recognize the freshman would grow into a beauty as she grew into herself. For now, she was definitely not the type he would roll with. She was too young and he had a firm policy of not "robbing the cradle."

She was sitting at the front of the art class taking notes, respectfully paying attention to Dr. Pierre Louise. Someone on the project team had to be the notetaker and information arranger. While he considered others that he watched in the classroom, he couldn't take his eyes off the freshman beauty with the librarian "get back" glasses on. By the end of the class, the librarian had won.

As soon as class was over, he approached her. "Hello, my name is Brandon Johnson and I want to be in your project group."

The dark beauty peered at him over the top of those thick glasses. "Excuse me. Have we met?"

Brandon held out his hand. "I'm Brandon. And you are?"

She slowly put her hand in his. "Altha Harkens."

"We've met now. I want to be in your group for the art project. Let me guess…you're a Physics, Engineering or Pre-Med major?"

She frowned. "Pre-med."

"Ah ha. Pre-med. I knew because you were taking some serious notes. I do best around detail-oriented people and together we can get the project done right. Let me know by the next class on Wednesday."

Brandon started to walk away, then heard her firm tone call after him. "If I'm bringing the notes, exactly what do you have to offer the group?"

He froze mid-step, turned and placed his hand on his chest in feigned indignation. He declared, "Sister, don't you know? I am the Art Aficionado. Art is my thing, but of more importance, I have transportation to take our group wherever it needs to go to earn an A on the project." He smiled a million-dollar smile that made Altha and the ladies sitting next to her begin to laugh at his boldness.

The next day, Brandon was sitting with a group of friends in the Manley Student Center when he saw Altha walk in. He walked up to her and in his most charming voice said, "So, are you going to let me in? Do I get to be on your team?" He gave her a winning smile and a wink.

Altha put a hand on her hip and pursed her lips together.

Brandon put a hand on his chest in feigned shock. "I can't even imagine you not wanting me on your team. Did you forget? I am the Art…"

His group of friends and fraternity brothers finished his sentence and shouted out loud for all to hear, "Aficionado!"

Altha broke into a smile and giggled. When she smiled, Brandon knew he was on the team. He flashed yet another smile, but thought to himself, *Let me stop playing with this freshman girl. She's far too young for me.* He made himself look away from her hidden beauty.

Altha looked him in the eye with so much seriousness. "I'm serious about my grades. I took this course for an easy A to balance out my science courses. I didn't realize this A wouldn't be easy. I expect you to be serious about the project."

He put his hand on his chest. "Serious as a heart attack."

She gave him a shy smile. "So how did you become the Art Aficionado? Should I be checking your references?"

Brandon feigned shock again. He had to smile at the boldness of this young freshman. "I'll tell you the story one day, while we're working on the project. I promise you have nothing to worry about. I'll take your grades, and this project seriously."

He could understand her concern about him not taking the project seriously. He knew he came across as carefree and playful.

Truth was, he worked hard and played hard, but before he played, he worked hard. This simple approach to college was effective. He was graduating as a member of Phi Beta Kappa Honors society which made his mother proud. He was initiated into his father's fraternity as a junior which made his father proud.

One might assume he was arrogant, yet those who knew him best understood how thankful and quietly humble he was. He lived by the Golden Rule and got on his knees every night in thanks for his family and every morning in thanks for a new day. One unique trait that spoke of his coming greatness was his ability to listen to people in a way that made the person feel special and the center of his attention.

Altha nodded, spied at him with curious eyes for a moment, then walked away.

As he watched the gentle sway of her hips. he thought to himself, *Now that's a serious sister indeed.*

   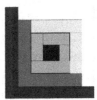

CHAPTER 8

HER ART AFICIONADO

Altha was shocked to see Brandon after all these years. And in Dublin especially. She wouldn't have been surprised to run into him in Atlanta, but how did he find himself in her small hometown? The look on his face let her know he was fondly remembering their first meeting and their time together working on their art project his last year at Morehouse and her first year at Spelman. She had her own fond memories of that time.

* * *

She couldn't believe he was picking her up in a candy apple red, BMW 325. After having her head buried in her books for her challenging science classes, she welcomed the opportunity to take a ride in a nice car with a nice, good looking man on this beautiful spring day.

So far, they and the rest of their team had traveled to a Buckhead art gallery that was a private home for a display on Haitian bead art. They visited the Atlanta airport and focused on expansive pieces there, and delved into the underground scene in the Midtown warehouse district to visit artist workshops. Altha had a new understanding of the vitality, history, tradition and culture that made Atlanta the darling of the South.

Today, it was just the two of them, riding through Atlanta with the top of his convertible down, headed to the High Museum of Art. When she first got in the car, Brandon was blasting Alecia Keys spring hit, "I Need You," which seemed to play on every radio station at the same time. Brandon was singing along with his deep baritone and Altha wondered whether he was flirting with her, or if he just liked the song.

After he glanced over at her a few times, she became acutely aware of his handsomeness. She needed to keep him and herself focused on the reason they were going to the museum and stop the flood of emotions that was surely brought on by the beauty of the day, the ride in the convertible and this chocolate man singing this intimate song. She decided to start a conversation.

"So, you promised to give me your references that support your claim of being the Art Aficionado."

Brandon laughed and reached over to turn the radio down. "You're still doubting me? What must I do to prove myself?"

"You said you'd tell me the story."

Brandon sat there, thoughtful for a moment, seemingly deciding whether he wanted to cross the line of their being team partners to share personal information about himself. He finally took a deep breath. "My mom, who I adore, is an art teacher."

Altha nodded thoughtfully. That made sense. His eye for art and the way he had explained some of the pieces they had seen on their outings was impressive. She had been wondering where that came from.

"She's taken me to some of the finest museums in America and Europe, first as her unwilling partner, but after a while, I loved our 'art adventures.' My dad, a dentist, was happy to finance our trips, but wanted no parts of her art outings. He was happy that

I eventually enjoyed going with her because it gave him a break from it.

"She always made it a fun time of discovery for me. She would place me in front of a great work of art and with her calming voice, would share through her seasoned eyesight what she saw on a canvas or in a sculpture."

Altha stared at Brandon, beginning to see him through different eyes.

"After a while, she stopped telling me what she saw and would ask me for my take on a piece of art. She used to put her chin on his shoulder and whisper, 'See what I see, my little Art Aficionado.' I loved it when she did that. Through those experiences, she began to direct and educate my artistic eye. So even though I say it jokingly, my mom, Mayola Johnson, qualified me to be the Art Aficionado."

Altha had to smile, with completely new appreciation for Brandon. But his story had done little to distract her from what felt like a growing attraction. She needed to put a stop to the emotions stirring within her. Brandon had already told her he had received early acceptance to Wharton's school of Business for his MBA. After graduation, he was leaving for Philadelphia. Not that he would be interested in her anyway, if he wasn't.

They moved through the exhibit at the High Museum of Art, Brandon explaining what he saw in the different pieces of art that caught his eye. Altha was scribbling copious notes as he spoke. She was glad she had accepted him on her team. Not only would she get her A, but he had made it a most enjoyable experience.

They reached a far corner of the building on the lower level and there, Altha, the budding scientist, had a life-changing, art experience. She almost passed by the piece, but something about it called to her. Immediately knowing it would work for the team project, she prepared to get information to share with the group. Standing in a beam of sunlight, Altha began writing the description of the piece. It was a photo of a field of flowers and in the middle of the scene was a shoulder-up picture of a very dark-skinned, young woman in a white linen shirt. The young woman looked to be close to Altha's age.

Taking her usual scientist's approach, she began recording her data. The artist's name was Ruud Van Empel, a Dutch photographer from Amsterdam. The title was *Analogy #1*. The size of the piece was 39.4 x 30.3 inches. The art medium used was photography, and the colors included...

(Analogy #1 Reprinted with permission from Ruud Van Empel)

As she was about to describe the colors, Altha felt the warmth of Brandon's presence right behind her. Before she could turn around, he placed his hands on her waist in a respectful manner. With gentle pressure, he kept her turned forward, looking at the piece of art.

He placed his chin on her shoulder—as if he had done it a thousand times before.

"See what I see…" He spoke in a whisper and the feeling of his breath against her neck combined with his Terre D'Hermes fragrance distracted her. Altha had been around men before. She had a boyfriend in high school and a number of freshman at Morehouse were showing interest. But there was something about Brandon's touch that stunned her. It was seasoned and wise, patient and safe.

Altha began to feel lightheaded. She searched for the right words to describe the bubbling of light that rose out of her chest that made her gasp, then overflowed onto her shoulders to cascade down the rest of her body. She was frozen, not in fear, but in the rapture of his touch and presence.

She knew now how close Zora Neal Hurston, her favorite author, had come to describing this novel, youthful, life energy. Altha felt what Zora meant in *Their Eyes Were Watching God*, when she described pear blossoms and how the character, Janie, saw them. "…dust bearing bees sink into the sanctum of the bloom; the thou-sand sister-calyxes arch to meet the love embrace and the ecstatic shiver of the tree from root to tiniest branch creaming in every blossom and frothing with delight."

Altha hadn't arched like the limbs on Zora's pear trees, but she was definitely blooming and overflowing in delight due to Brandon's closeness.

Before she could move away, his quiet, deep words penetrated her emotional cloud. His soothing voice was easy to listen to. He reverently spoke her name, "Altha, in your notes, you are perfectly tactical and technical. Your descriptions of the physical dimensions, like length and width, colors and materials used are exact and detailed. But each piece says so much more than the physical. Stand with me and let me help you 'See what I see…..'"

Brandon began his lesson." Don't look only at the photo, look at our life in the present. It's the morning on a brilliant spring day in Atlanta, Georgia. Life is new and the world is calling us to do great things. We have unlimited potential, and our lives are just beginning. We are taking steps to make our dreams a reality."

He declared with confidence, "You will be a great doctor one day, but for today, see the natural sunlight streaming in on us, sharing its warmth. Hear the silence and stillness surrounding us, as if the building itself doesn't want to allow the world's outside sounds to intrude on what this piece of art is trying to say to us."

His soulful hypnosis continued, "Don't see the physical make-up of the piece. See the image for its details. Although the young woman is positioned in the center of the piece, don't engage your eyes there first. Look with me on the outer parts of the picture, on the background and together, we will work our vision towards its center subject. We will save the woman and meet her last." His words were crystal clear and played a melody on her rigid, science-based mindset as he implored her again to, "See what I see."

Altha followed his instructions. She saw that the background was bright and made up of images of pastels in a spring meadow. There were white tulips, pink poppies and white roses. Having been raised with country gardens, she recognized Camilla roses and fresh blooming yellow yarrow. Combined, they sang of springtime and newness. Her vision seemed to find an even deeper level of detail as she began to notice butterflies and bumblebees. The photo finishing almost made them seem alive, and in the intensity of Altha's gaze, she thought she saw a butterfly move its wing.

She fell even deeper into the photo. The meadow was now alive to her, and the flowers were moving as she pulled away from the periphery towards the center focus point of the photo. Her eyes, growing used to seeing life on this level, moved from the multiple pastels and fell onto the soothing darkness of the young woman. Her skin, in contrast with the bright pastel flowers, was an arrestingly black. In physics lab, they called it vonda black—a black so deep, it absorbs all color and reflects none. A black conceptually the color of space, absent the stars and as close as obtainable to the original darkness from which God spoke the creation.

While the woman's skin was dark, contrasting its flowered pastel surroundings, it had no blemishes and was perfect in its even tone. Altha's attention on the woman's eyes was fleeting at first, but then she absorbed the full weight of the woman's expression. Though young, she had a defiant look that showed no signs of weakness. It wasn't a scowl, but there was no doubt that she was strong enough to do anything and would not back down from any trial life would present.

There, standing in front of the photo of the young Black woman in the springtime meadow, Altha's breathing quickened as the message from the photo finally hit home. She understood now that the dark, smooth-skinned woman was not there for contrast with the flowery pastel background. She was there in the center of the springtime field and the focus of the piece because the woman, was in fact, the most exotic, God-given beautiful blossom of them all.

Altha had been able to block the world out. There was just the melody and dialogue between her and the photo. The image's tender message had been silently written upon her heart. She was a beautiful, unique person, who possessed the determination to conquer all the challenges in her world with defiant grace. That revelation, now manifest, settled on her and tears welled up in her eyes, slightly obscuring her vision and breaking, in part, the art piece's spell over her.

As she blinked and wiped her eyes, she realized she was standing alone. The warmth of Brandon's body and his hands on her waist were gone. There was no whispered voice guiding her thoughts.

Altha quickly turned around, wiping a tear from her right eye. She took in a cleansing breath to gather her composure. That's when she saw him. The one and only Brandon T. Johnson, sitting on a bench, legs crossed and leaning back watching her. His smile showed his confidence in knowing he had just successfully guided her onto a new level of vision in life. There was no denying Altha Harkens had just had her first true art experience.

Brandon's smile grew as he raised his arms in the air, pointed down at himself and broke the silence to confidently say, "I am The Art…"

Altha smiled. "…Aficionado."

That was over eleven years ago and yet Brandon still had the ability to elicit that same smile from her. She took a few steps back. "Goodness, I didn't recognize you at first, but it's you, Brandon T. Johnson, in the flesh. The Art Aficionado himself. "

He reached out to give her a friendly hug. The hug was too short and polite for her to swoon, but if Altha had, it would have been justified. Before her was not the 6' 2" slim, smooth faced pretty boy business executive to be. Brandon appeared to be a solid, self-assured man. He looked taller and as if he had added thirty pounds of muscle. His face now had a beard, his hair was tight and the glasses fit his studious look. The eye-catching, candy apple red BMW was replaced by a more modest Lincoln SUV.

It took her a minute to find her words. "What are you doing in Dublin?"

He took a deep breath. "Kind of taking a time out."

"I told you so." Jameli giggled.

Altha had gotten so caught up in the memories, she had forgotten the little girl was there, standing right next to her, holding her hand.

"I'm visiting my aunt, Lilly Baker. Wow, so you're the doctor Jameli couldn't stop talking about." He too looked at Jameli like the memories of their past made him forget all about her. He shook his head in pleasant surprise. "I'm happy to see that your dreams have come true."

"Thanks." Altha smiled, knowing she was blushing. Her curiosity was piqued. What did Brandon and Jameli mean by a time out?

The look in his eyes when he said it let her know it wasn't a conversation for standing in the yard with Jameli right there.

Before she could say anything he asked, "Do you practice here in Dublin?"

She shook her head. "No, I work at a hospital in Atlanta. I'm just in Dublin this week visiting. My sister's baby shower is on Saturday. I decided to take some extra time to spend with my mom and others here in the community."

Before either of them could speak, Jameli said, "Daddy, I'm hungry. Are we going home?" She hopped off the step and ran into the yard.

Brandon followed her with his eyes. "I guess I should get her home and feed her."

Altha laughed. "We fed her snacks, but I guess she needs some real food."

Altha wasn't ready to let him go. She had so many questions. Where was Jameli's mother? Did he realize his dreams of becoming a business executive as he had planned? What was this time out?

Before she could stop herself, Altha said, "Would you believe little ole' Dublin, Georgia just got their first Starbucks? Would you like to have coffee tomorrow afternoon? We can catch up on everything that's happened since college. I'm sure you have stories to tell."

Brandon looked surprised. She knew it was because asking him out for coffee was out of character for Altha, the shy freshman.

"Ummm...yeah...that sounds good. I teach at the local high school and also run an after school, boys-to-men transition group. But I can be available late afternoon early evening."

They traded phone numbers then parted, agreeing to meet up at 5pm the next day.

Before going in for dinner with her mom, Altha took a slow walk in her back yard near the white blossoming pear trees and had to smile, shaking her head in disbelief at having met the new

Brandon T. Johnson. He was as handsome as ever. Before she let her feelings go anywhere, she had to find out what was going on in his life.

She walked among the trees for a while, taking in deep breaths of the fresh country air. Her thoughts eventually drifted back to the list of possibilities for why her community had such a low pregnancy death rate. Perhaps the answer lay somewhere amongst the topics of slavery, 'haints and spirits,' healing spring water and birthing rings. If it were there, Altha was determined to ferret it out. By the time she reached the porch, she had a plan for solving the mystery of the medical safety zone and why pregnant Black women in her community seemed to do better than the rest of the pregnant Black women in the state of Georgia.

CHAPTER 9

✳ ✳ ✳

Soul Sister Sleuth

Altha awakened to the smell of a country breakfast and her mother humming in the kitchen. She smiled as she entered and walked to where her mother stood, finishing the last of the food preparations. She gave her mother a big hug, then went to have a seat at the table. It was obvious her mother was happy to have a guest.

After the meal, over two cups of steaming coffee, they shared their plans for the day. After some chores, Altha planned on solving part of the medical mystery that had her so intrigued. She mentioned the places she would go and the people she would see to conduct her research.

When she mentioned meeting Brandon at Starbucks, her mother's eyebrows raised.

"What? What's the problem?" Altha asked.

"Brandon is such a kind man who has been a major help to the young men in this community. He's done so much and everyone in the community has grown to love him in the year that he's been here."

"Okay…" Altha said slowly, wondering what her mother wasn't saying. She didn't have to wonder long.

"So what are your intentions with the young man?"

Altha laughed. "My intentions? What do you mean by intentions?"

Her mother sipped her coffee slowly. "When was the last time you had coffee with a young man?"

Altha shrugged, not wanting to admit to herself how long it had been. "It's nothing like that. We just want to sit and talk, catch up." She explained briefly that they had done a project together in college.

Her mother raised an eyebrow. "A lot of things start off with just talking. In fact, your father and I started off just talking." The twinkle in her eye let Altha know she was reliving some sweet memories. With love in her voice, she said, "Altha you know the highest form of intimacy is communication."

Altha stood and hugged her mother whispering, "Thanks mom." She kissed Annabelle's cheek on the way back to her room to dress for the day.

Altha's route began in downtown Dublin. By 10 a.m., she was parked and walking across the Dublin City Square past the confederate soldier statue. She climbed the Greek-columned courthouse steps, entered the front door and followed the signs to the county court records room. Upon entering, she was greeted by the smile of the venerable Mrs. Anne Jordan, a stately, brown-skinned, sixty-year-old with greying temples and intelligent eyes.

Along with being a city clerk, Mrs. Jordan was the *de facto* local town historian. Altha knew if anyone could explain the impact of slavery on the community, it would be her. As Altha laid out the mystery of the medical safety zone for her, Mrs. Jordan's spectacled eyes were inquisitive as she listened intently. Mrs. Jordan confirmed for Altha that although she had known of infants that didn't make it during childbirth, she was hard pressed to think of a local Black woman who died in the period surrounding childbirth.

When Altha presented the theory on it being the result of slavery and breeding, Mrs. Jordan listened patiently, but disagreed. She displayed an encyclopedic knowledge of the goings and comings of people in the Dublin area. She spoke of a migration North in the 1890's, following the breakdown of Black progress after the post-Civil War Reconstruction period. She gave examples of the harsh Jim Crow laws that were established to take back the newly-gained freedoms from Blacks. She described how even more local Black folks left to go to the big cities in the 1920's to avoid the heavy social backlash that included the rebirth of the Klan and a second wave of oppression for Black citizens.

These comments gave way to short stories of the great Black migration of the 30's and 40's, when families moved to Detroit and Chicago as America turned from an agricultural to an industrial workforce. As she listened, Altha was reminded of two great uncles, both Harkens, who left the Dublin area to go up to Detroit. The last remaining uncle, Uncle Rev, even at nearly ninety, still returned to Dublin for the Byrdhill Baptist church homecomings each third Sunday in September.

Mrs. Jordan hammered down her point that at almost 200 years removed and many generations away from slavery, any protection would have broken down over the years. The slavery theory collapsed entirely as Mrs. Jordan posed the question, "If the protection of the mothers was due to slavery, why does it seem to stop at our community's boundaries?"

Altha had to agree that the patterns didn't fit and thanked Mrs. Jordan for her time. As she left the courthouse to return to her car, she refocused her thoughts onto the "haints" theory. If the protection was from spirits, the logical place to answer more questions was at the spiritual center of her community, Byrdhill Baptist Church. She knew just the person to approach, the Holy Ghost-filled, senior deacon, J.T. Edmond, who had been old when Altha was young, but seemed to never age.

Altha recollected how the belief in haints and spirits was a hold-over from slavery, but was ingrained in African American traditions and folklore. More spirits than ghosts, haints could protect people or injure them, but were controlled by what folks called "roots." These roots were special medicines and poultices that could heal any malady. Today, root healers would be considered herbalists and natural healers.

Altha reminisced as she rolled into the gravel parking lot of a small brick and mortar country church, white steeple included. The lot had a dozen cars owned by the participants in the regular Wednesday noon Bible Study. As she stepped from her car, she saw the fields around the church were plowed and had green cotton shoots rising.

The church was started after slavery when newly freed slaves met each Sunday for services under a muscadine vine by a small creek on the edge of the property. Byrdhill Baptist church had burned down twice, once from a lightning strike and once during the 1920's under mysterious circumstances. The current structure had a modern kitchen and fellowship hall with an indoor baptismal pool. Despite the modern air conditioning, church fans with funeral home advertisements were tucked next to well-worn Bibles and hymnals into the back of each wooden pew.

As she entered the sanctuary, she heard a beautiful, piercing, aged tenor voice leading a hymn that sailed out of the windows and doors and blessed the church grounds. Deacon J.T.'s final phrase of his signature gospel song, filled with emotion, took flight.

"Oh, Jesus! Will fix it...for you..."

The Bible study members said, "Amen" and began rising to leave.

Deacon J.T. Edmond was over eighty years old and had eyes that were sharp and sparkled with enthusiasm for life. His skin was dark and smooth, and his grey hair was cut close. He was bowlegged and was about 6'2" before age bent him over, yet he was active and still on fire for the Lord.

Deacon J.T.'s most exceptional trait was his ability to listen and talk with people of all ages. He was patient with the youngest children in the flock and Altha could remember having Sunday talks with Deacon J.T. all her life. He would listen quietly, with a look of concentration on his face, while rubbing his rough, work hands together. His first words were always a probing question that let her know he was listening. Next he would repeat back what she said in a simplified form before he would give an answer. His advice was always thoughtful, but all his conversations ended the same with him saying through a smile, "I'll put it on my prayer list."

The spry Deacon J.T. shouted, "Halleluiah!" as he walked toward Altha with outstretched arms, crying out, "Doctor Girl come here." Deacon J.T. hugged her, rocking her from side to side. It reminded her of the warmth and acceptance her father's hugs held. It was manly, respectful, safe, yet sincere in Christian love.

As she helped him pick up the sanctuary and begin to lock up the church, Altha told him about the medical safety zone mystery and her list that included slavery, haints, the healing spring water and birthing rings.

As was his habit, he repeated back exactly what her question was to make sure he understood. He admitted he fetched water each first of the month for his wife as she carried his two daughters during pregnancy, God rest her soul. And his brother, Lou, owned the property where the healing spring was located, and over the years was responsible for making some of the birthing rings. Deacon J.T. knew the traditions and did believe the spring water had healing properties, but as for haints, he knew a thing or two about them as well.

He first heard stories of haints from his mother, Magnolia, when he was small. Even now, on rare occasions, he was asked by some of the older members to bless a home or plot of land to ward off the spirits. The color blue scared away haints, as they could not cross waters. Locally, most porch ceilings were painted a light "haint blue." Bottle trees with yellow and blue bottles could capture lingering bad haints at night and hold them in the bottle until the day's sunlight destroyed them.

Altha thought of the blue bottle trees at her home that were a constant in her mother's gardens over the years. She also thought of the light blue on her porch ceiling now realizing there was a reason behind the color.

Placing salt on the doorstep could ward them off. In addition, putting straws in a corner of a room would distract the haint from entering the house fully and causing mischief. A large mirror at the front door entrance was a sure-fire way to protect the home.

Root healers or naturalists in the community used poultices and good luck charms to keep haints at bay. Deacon J.T. recounted firsthand how he had been burned in a fire at the age of seven and how the local healer was the only one around to give care as they didn't have a modern doctor. There was a Whites-only hospital twelve miles away that would sometimes see Blacks after hours. For the most part, the early treatment of emergency injuries on the farm was done by a family member or the root healer.

Deacon J.T. became more animated as he described how the old woman healer created a poultice of spider webs, spices and a cream. The healer put the cream on his leg, then lay the spiderweb concoction on it before wrapping it. His recall was crystal clear as he spoke that he didn't start feeling better until the woman began to pray over and "talk the fire" out of the burn. As she spoke, he could feel a coolness come over the burn and it stopped hurting. The old man lifted his leg, showing a healed burn wound the size of a grapefruit. When Altha saw the impressive size of the healed burn, she couldn't imagine it healing in modern days without a hospital admission and antibiotics.

Try as he might, Deacon J.T. could not remember any root healing or haint protections out of the ordinary that could help to better a pregnant woman's outcome. He conjectured that maybe the women's faith in Jesus helped, as they were part of a praying community. The only things he knew for a fact were the traditions about bringing the mother the special spring water each first of the month and the birthing rings. He laughed as he added with a wry smile, "And you don't start relations with your wife until they finish her birthing quilt."

Altha heard the last comment, but was absorbed in realizing that the haints were not the cause of the medical safety zone. As she waved goodbye, Altha blushed as Deacon J.T. said, "I'm so proud of you and everything you've accomplished. And I'll put your question on my prayer list."

That evening, after a cup of coffee with Brandon, she planned to visit Deacon J.T.'s brother, Lou's, property to pursue the remaining active theories on the list—the healing spring water and birthing rings.

CHAPTER 10

* * *

MAGIC RINGS AND HEALING SPRINGS

A ltha stopped by home to shower and change before heading to the Starbucks to meet Brandon. As she entered the house, her mother reminded her the next day she would need to make a run over to her godmother, Mrs. Evelynn's, to drop off some slices of pound cake for a women's bridge reception.

Altha went to her room and looked at herself in the full-length mirror in her old bedroom. She reminisced and saw a slim, thirteen-year-old with glasses morph into an eighteen-year-old young woman that transitioned into a college graduate who faded into a distinguished doctor. She admired her reflection of a confident woman who had accomplished goals. She marveled how at each stage in her life, this same mirror had called out the best in her.

She chose a form-fitting, blue sundress and sandals and decided to wear her contact lenses instead of her glasses. She smiled as she liked what she saw in the old mirror.

When Altha drove into the Starbucks parking lot, she saw Brandon talking to three young men who looked like students. If things hadn't changed too much since her teenage days, they were probably on their way to play basketball at the local Boys Club, a converted feed house. The boys would be joined there by a flock of young girls who would watch the league play. Once she had been in that flock of girls. She smiled warmly at the memory. Brandon turned and waved as she exited her car. He shook each young brother's hand, then turned towards Altha.

Brandon's biceps were straining his blue, polo shirt and he wore jeans, and white and red Nike runners. As she approached him, he extended his hand in a semiformal way. Her hand seemed to blend into his warm, firm handshake. They entered the coffee shop and decided to sit outside.

Brandon went to place their orders as Altha sat and looked anew at downtown Dublin. Not much had changed structurally in terms of new buildings, but there was a new youthfulness and energy to Dublin. The local community hospital had been recently renovated and there were trucking, lumber, pulp, and chalk companies. Also driving the economy were numerous local state parks, and traffic from students and supporters of Georgia Southern University.

Brandon joined her with their orders and the focus of their small talk was his beautiful, talented daughter, Jameli. He joked that when he sent her to college, he was going to get her some of those thick, black "don't mess with me glasses," like Altha the freshman had. They laughed at the thought of how serious Altha was as she began college.

With the ice broken, their conversation flowed like two old friends. Brandon encouraged Altha to shared how she chose medical school on the West Coast. She explained her decision to stay out West for anesthesia training, knowing she would have to gravitate back within driving distance of Dublin to settle down to support her mother. She shared her travel history and confided that she still found solace in art museums, having visited Paris and Rome right after medical school. She excitedly revealed a recent purchase of her first serious art investment.

"Hmmmm, so the Art Aficionado left a lasting mark on you, huh?" Brandon teased.

Altha blushed. "Yeah, I guess he did." She took a sip of her coffee and gave him a rewarding smile.

Altha had to catch herself when she realized how relaxed she felt sharing with him. Something was different about Brandon. He was an excellent listener. His expressions, body language, and intense eye contact showed he was right there with her, present in the moment and attentive. His broad smile showed that he understood her humor, while his questions showed that he was actively following what she said. It was refreshing that there was no intellectual one up-manship, or any effort to make his views dominate the conversation.

Altha found it easy to talk with him and the conversation flowed like the waters along a lazy creek bed, going where it could, gently flowing around any harder topics, but moving with the certainty of one of nature's unstoppable forces.

When the talk turned to his history, Brandon explained with a stiff upper lip how after college, he experienced a series of losses, then gains, and then losses. Altha was amazed at his resiliency. She couldn't believe the life of the clean-cut Brandon, who sported a BMW and was headed to Wharton School of Business, had changed so drastically from what he expected.

She listened with empathy as he described the loss of his parents and how it landed him in the Peace Corps in Kenya. She loved his stories of experiencing Kenyan culture, until he got to the tragedy of losing his wife and unborn baby. The "time out" he and Jameli were on finally made sense.

Altha remembered the look on Mrs. Baker's face when she asked the sewing group the question about knowing anyone who passed away during childbirth. Mrs. Baker's question asking if the person had to be from Dublin now made sense.

"So along with being dad to Jameli, I teach Home Economics, Business Calculus and Geography at the local high school. I also started the men's program I mentioned. Those boys in the parking lot you saw recently joined the team."

Altha was fascinated that Brandon was so actively engaged in the community. He was a testimony to the impact that a man with focus could have.

As Brandon stood to go get their second round of coffee and some sugar cookies, Altha shook her head. Brandon was doing so much for their community in Dublin. He sounded so busy. If this was a time out, how hard had he been working in Kenya?

She winced, thinking of the losses he had suffered. Her mind instantly flashed back to Carlton Murphy screaming the past weekend as he agonized over the possible loss of his wife. She was lost in thought and pained at the realization that Brandon had experienced those same exact emotions. She didn't notice Brandon returning until he sat down.

Brandon studied her for a moment. "I hope my story didn't bring you down. Sorry. It's hard to tell my history without mentioning the tragedies." He paused for a second and said, "I just want to be open and truthful with you."

Altha shook her head. "Your story didn't depress me. Instead, I'm sincerely impressed with you. I remember who you were back then and where your life has ended up is amazing. I'm sorry for all the pain you went through, but your life is a…testimony. Your resilience is…inspiring."

Brandon laughed. "Yeah, I was pretty full of myself back then." He stared into space for a moment. "Life has a way of humbling you."

Altha said, "Interestingly, I came home early because of a challenging case that involved a delivery and the attempt to save a Black mother's life."

Brandon listened as Altha told him about Tasha Murphy's case. She shared about her research and what she had discovered about the patient's risk factors for her outcome. She had to gather herself as she shared that the risk factor that surprised her the most was the fact that she was a Black woman in Georgia. Brandon was shocked when he heard that Black women were dying at three times the average rate in America and that his home state had the worst rate of them all.

He shook his head. "I had always assumed that if I had brought Neema back to America to deliver, there would have been no chance for the tragedy to happen. Now I'm not so sure." He was silent for a moment. "That's so hard to believe. I just thought it was because of the medical system in Kenya. How can this be happening right here in the United States?"

Altha's expression changed from despair and anger to determination when she shared with Brandon the mystery of the medical safety zone here in Dublin. He was engrossed as she revealed there had not been any reported deaths of Black women during childbirth in their community in many years. Brandon leaned forward in focused concentration and urged her on in her discussion.

She shared everything she had learned during her research online and her visits to find out more about slavery and spirits. When she told Brandon she was going to check out the healing spring water after their coffees, Brandon cut her off. "I'm in!"

Altha hadn't thought of having a partner while working up the mystery. She remembered how great they had worked together on their college project. She smiled and said, "So are you asking to be on my project team again?"

Brandon laughed. "I guarantee that together, we'll do the same A plus work."

His smooth voice moved her, and as his beautiful full lips in slow motion parted to say the word "together," Altha began spiraling.

She quickly looked away from Brandon, hoping she wasn't blushing, as a warm light long dormant in her bosom pulsed.

Oh no! Is this brother about to make me swoon again? Altha hoped he hadn't noticed her tremble of excitement before she regained her composure.

They left Altha's car at the Starbucks and drove Brandon's car to investigate the healing spring at Uncle Lou's. It was a short drive, but as if the soul music gods knew the two old friends were together, Alicia Keys' song, "I Need You" from Spring 2007 came on the radio. They were both flowing with the music, thinking back to the red BMW convertible that was Brandon's calling sign. They thought back to a time before each had struck out into the world to claim their success. Together, the two old friends swayed to the beat, looking at each other as they joined Alicia Keys in singing one of the song's hooks together, *"Hey! Hey! Hey!"*

Pulling up to the front of the property, they were greeted by a warm yellow ranch home with a well-manicured front lawn. The home's flower beds had white and red azaleas in the front. Dogwood, plum, and fig trees bordered the property lines. A two-story magnolia tree decorated with its oversized white blossoms was in the front right corner of the lawn and held court over the seeming thousands of other blossoming flowers.

Next to a well-worn path that led back to the spring was a functional but rusty swing set, obviously left standing in kindness to the children who might come for infrequent visits. The swing set was straddled by two more flower beds with white roses, red tulips, yellow daffodils and a pair of five-feet hydrangea bushes that put forth large, baby blue, puffed flowers, each one large enough to easily fill Altha's palm.

Altha and Brandon exited the car and walked up a path past a small slate rock with the words, "Help yourself. God is good" written on it. Halfway back, the path curved, splitting between two, well-cared for muscadine vines, one with golden drops and the other with rich purple drops. It was too early in the year for muscadines, but the leaves of both vines seemed to reflect the care and exceptional nutrients found in the soil and water on this land.

In back of the house was a garage that held lawn mowers new and old. Attached to the garage was a small workshop with open windows. As they approached, they could see someone on a workbench and could hear the sounds of woodwork interspersed with the light humming of a church hymn familiar to Altha. Each step closer enveloped her and Brandon in the warmth of a happy baritone humming most lines and only singing the chorus, "It is Well with My Soul."

The barking of a hound dog alerted the woodworker to his visitors and the workshop door filled with a tall, slender man in overalls. He was older than Deacon J.T., but there was something familiar about his smile and warm disposition. As one of the oldest men in the church Lou Edmond affectionately called Uncle Lou by all church members. He was Deacon J.T's older brother and there was no denying that, but while the deacon had a full smile, Uncle Lou had lost a couple of teeth. It didn't detract from his dimples and spry looking eyes.

As Altha approached Uncle Lou, she saw the goodness that seemed to beam from his smiling face and his weather worn skin.

"Welcome! Altha, your mother and J.T. told me you were back home. It's good to see you girl. Can I get you something to drink?" His voice was high and raspy.

Altha walked up and gave him a hug. His overalls smelled of fresh woodwork, and flecks of oak dust were on his pants leg. She turned to introduce Brandon who gave Deacon Lou, recognizing him from church, a firm Christian handshake with no wavering of the eyes between them, that spoke of two men who knew themselves.

She had read the sign about helping herself, but proper home training told her to be polite and ask Uncle Lou if it was okay to get some of the water from the spring before asking him some questions. Uncle Lou handed her two cups and waved them on with a smile, encouraging them to get as much as they needed.

Before she could get back to the trail, Uncle Lou, shouted, "My Lord!"

Altha and Brandon were startled and stopped and turned.

The old man looked at them and said, "You two are one of the most handsome couples I have seen in years. Your babies are going to be beautiful."

Altha was taken aback by the misunderstanding. "No, Deacon

Lou, Brandon is just a friend from college. We just started working on a project together today. We're not married and I'm not pregnant."

Uncle Lou shook his head, as if what she said passed in one ear and out the other. "You two are blessed! Y'all gonna have some beautiful Black babies." He then continued into the house waving his arm in the air. "Stop by before you leave now. I got something for you."

Altha looked at Brandon and shrugged as he laughed and urged her down the path towards the spring.

She said, "The spring water is supposed to be healing water. My dad was convinced that if one drank the spring water, they would live forever." Altha pressed her lips together at the irony of her father's untimely passing. She wished his words had been true.

Before they stepped into the entrance into the woods, Altha could feel a comforting, cool breeze that welcomed them into the forest. Twenty yards further down the path was the cement cistern from which the fresh, healing spring water rose. The cistern was a cement cylinder that had been placed to guide the spring water that filled it and ran over its sides to create a small stream that ran further into the woods to join a small brook.

The tree coverage of the forest seemed to create a canopy of shade that separated the space into a natural inner sanctum. It was quiet, and the bubbling of the spring and the brook were the background sounds for the occasional wild bird call. The scene could have been a painting and captured the peace in nature while glowing with an aura of the spiritual.

As Altha thought of the hundreds of men over the decades who had made this trek, a single ray of light penetrated the forest roof and seemed to land on the spring, making it glow against a background of various shades of green foliage. She followed the path and moved onto the steppingstones that allowed one to get next to the spring in the cistern.

She lifted the screen used to keep out the leaves and gracefully bent, seeing through the clear water down to the spring's bubbling sandy bottom. She gently dipped a cup deep into the cistern. Immediately, she noticed how cool the water was and dipped further almost to arm's length down before she turned the cup up to fill it.

She stood and handed Brandon the cold cup of healing water and then scooped out a cup for herself. As she stepped back off the stones onto solid ground, Altha raised her glass, eyeing Brandon to toast. Brandon raised his cup to hers and Altha declared, "To healing!"

Brandon said, "*Kuponya*. It means, 'Be healed' in Swahili."

Eyeing each other in the intimate shadows of the forest, the two slowly drank together. The pure water was cool and refreshing. Altha didn't know if the effect was increased by the beauty of the shaded alcove or Brandon's company, but she felt good. Her knowledge that women over the years drank from this same spring made her feel a connection to home that she had not felt in years.

As Altha and Brandon headed up the path to return to the woodshop, both were reflective and silent as they took in the lushness of Uncle Lou's flower beds. He was standing in the doorway of his woodshop, smiling from ear to ear.

"I know you just had an experience that only God's spring water could give." He handed a clean gallon jug to Brandon. "Why don't you go back down to the spring and get some water for Mrs. Baker?"

Brandon thanked him and turned back to the spring as Altha and Uncle Lou began talking.

"Uncle Lou, do you think the spring water actually has healing properties?"

After a thoughtful pause, he answered, "I've seen many people healed in many ways by it."

"Where did the tradition of the men bringing their pregnant wives a glass of the spring water on the first of each month start?"

"My mother told me Stella, a local healer, started it many years ago. It was a tradition for generations, just like the tradition of giving women with child one of these handmade birthing rings."

Countless times as a child, Altha played with her mother's birthing ring, which was kept in a jewelry box. The ring carved of wood was two toned and smoothed to a fine finish. That simple wooden ring was given by her father the first time her mother was blessed to be with child. The ring was reused for the next four pregnancies. Her mother told her when a woman became with child, if she had a good husband, he would give the ring as a gift and begin bringing her monthly cups of the spring water.

She asked, "Do you think the water can protect mothers during birthing times?"

Uncle Lou spoke with affection, "Honey, I don't think so. According to my mama, toting spring water was started by Stella to help teach our young men to tend to the mothers of their children. The act of fetching water made the young men have to learn to think outside of themselves, and at least once a month for eight months, think of the special thing that woman was doing for him. So that tradition wasn't put there for the mothers. It was put there to quietly train the fathers." Uncle Lou winked.

Altha understood she was being let in on a family secret.

"Gifting pregnant women with a birthing ring was started by Stella too." He invited Altha into the woodshop. There on a polished tree branch on a base stand were hundreds of wooden rings of all sizes.

"The ring doesn't mean the couple was married, but was, by tradition, worn by the mother when she was found pregnant all through the delivery and until her quilt was finished. You might call it a friendship ring, a boyfriend, husband, and sometimes lover ring, but because it was worn while giving birth, most call it a birthing ring."

Uncle Lou picked up one of the rings, smoothing his finger over it. "The wood is special. It was struck by lightning and experienced the ultimate power of God and survived. They have a special energy to them." He drew Altha close to the collection. "Take one."

Altha couldn't resist his generosity and chose a dark-stained, oak ring whose hue blended with her skin tone and would require people to take a double look to see if it was there. After finding the right fit, she placed it in her pocket and hugged Uncle Lou. "Thank you. This has been a wonderful experience."

Brandon quietly returned to the shed with a peculiar expression on his face. He raised his jug of spring water and thanked Uncle Lou. He was pensive and quiet as they walked back out to the road.

Uncle Lou waved goodbye. "You two sure are a handsome couple. If your first child is a boy, be sure to name him after your daddy, Sonny. He was a good man, and that name deserves to live forever."

Altha waved back and smiled. Why was Uncle Lou insisting on them having babies? Was he seeing something about their future?

CHAPTER 11

✳ ✳ ✳

It Is Well – Ni Vizuri

The two novice investigators were quiet as they drove back to Starbucks so Altha could get her car. Brandon seemed unexpectedly silent. Altha respected his space and busied herself with the realization that she had not solved the mystery. She had no answers as to why women in her hometown did so well when right across the county line, pregnant Black women died at three times the normal rate.

They drove in silence with a vibe that was completely opposite from the Alicia Keys influenced energy they arrived with. Altha directed her attention to the natural beauty of the horizon and the evening's orange and purple filled sunset.

They arrived at her car and Brandon got out to open her door. She remembered he used to do the same when they rode in his BMW convertible. Ever the gentleman.

Although Brandon was still mute, Altha said, "Uncle Lou basically told me the spring water and ring traditions where meant more for the support team of men than for the pregnant mothers." She briefly shared what Uncle Lou had told her, then wondered aloud, "What kind of mind and foresight did it take to turn the spring water gestures into a tradition? Whoever this Stella was, she was pretty smart and is probably laughing down from heaven on how she trained generations of men to be attentive to the mothers of their offspring."

She had to admit that a single, kind gesture once a month could make all the difference and remind the men that as they lead a home, they also serve it. She may not have an answer to her medi-cal mystery, but she was thankful she got a birthing ring and some good, healing water out of the deal.

When she entered her car, she wondered about Uncle Lou's compliment. Had Uncle Lou seen a natural beauty when she was with Brandon? She chuckled to herself. *That baby will have to wait.*

She smiled as she waved to Brandon and started up her car. Before she could pull off, Brandon, who had been silent all the way back, jogged over and knocked on her window. When she rolled it down, he extended his hand. "Thanks for letting me on your team. Again." His broad smile warmed her heart.

On the way home, she turned up the music. Her thoughts went back to Uncle Lou's insistence on them having beautiful babies. He was right. Especially if they came out anything like Jameli.

That night, Altha struggled to sleep and couldn't decide whether or not she had a teenage swoon while around Brandon. She re-lived the intimate tasting of the water they shared and smiled at Uncle Lou's being sly like a fox by throwing out his embarrassing compliments.

It was obvious Brandon was off limits and still in a healing phase as testified by his unexpected silence while driving back to Starbucks. But try as she might to keep her thoughts of him in the friendship category, Altha couldn't help but link him to Zora's de-scription of nature's love.

She fell asleep to the whispering echoes of Zora's love phrases— *Bees...blooms... arched...love embrace ...ecstatic shiver...frothing with delight.*

The next morning, Altha arose and looked at herself in the

mirror. She turned to the side and imagined having a pregnant stomach. She pushed a pillow under her pajama top and looked at her profile again. She giggled and covered her mouth. "Not yet, kid."

She thought about her sister, Tee, who was due to give birth any day now. Tee had a glow and a calmness about her that seemed to soften her. How the two sisters still butted heads was beyond Altha.

Altha's mother gently knocked on the door, nearly catching Altha playing pregnant. She hid the pillow as the door eased open. Annabelle Harkens entered her bedroom and sat next to Altha.

"It's nice to have you home. I'm glad you moved back to Georgia." She smoothed her hand over Altha's. "The next couple of days will be exciting with the baby shower. And I can't wait until my first grandchild arrives!"

She looked Altha directly in the eye. "Please be sensitive to your little sister. Even though she's tough, she's fragile in many ways. You would be surprised at what people overcome in order to participate in this thing called life. While you are one of my smartest children, Tee is one of my toughest. There are some things you might learn from your younger sister. Please don't let the six years difference between you two become an ocean. Tee loves you, but doesn't always express it right."

Altha had to give it to her mom. She knew how to get to her. "I'll be nice, Mom. I promise. I'll be kinder during her birthing time. And I'll fall in line with all your plans for the shower. Whatever you need, I'm yours."

Her mother smiled and gave her a deep hug. In that moment, Altha was even more sure of her decision to move back to Georgia. There were no motherly hugs on the West Coast and this was something she needed in her life.

Her mother got up from the bed and walked to the door. "Don't forget to take the pound cake to Mrs. Evelynn's for the ladies bridge game."

✳ ✳ ✳

Brandon kept his eyes closed as he awakened from a deep, restful sleep. He lay still, ensuring he had entered full consciousness and had escaped his regular morning torture of a recurring nightmare. He was not convinced of the morning's grace until he heard the cooing of doves outside his window. He could hear his aunt starting breakfast and Jameli's cheerful sing-song voice, talking about her upcoming day.

It was the first time in a long time that he hadn't awakened because of a nightmare. He stared at the ceiling. He hadn't awakened feeling so much peace in years. A smile broke out on his face as he thanked God. He prayed that sweet sleep free of nightmares would continue and that he would awaken every morning with this level of peace.

His sleep and peace weren't the only things that had changed. Since Tuesday evening when he picked Jameli up from the Harkens' and saw Altha, Jameli had returned somewhat to her old, talkative, inquisitive self. She'd flooded him with questions like, "How did you know Dr. Altha? What was she like when she was young? Do you think I could be a doctor? When can we go to Spelman for a visit?"

Her new friendship with Altha was making the girl come alive. Even though Jameli was Swahili for, "a young girl who listens to old women," she was all talk now.

Brandon rolled over on his side, enjoying the morning banter between Jameli and his Aunt Lilly. His aunt was kind and was patient with him and Jameli. When they first arrived in Dublin, Jameli was withdrawn and quiet. His aunt welcomed her with love and with her seasoned skills of nurturing. Even though she was still quiet, Jameli began to blossom. The girl was academically excellent and was blowing away her classes while slowly making some friends.

Aunt Lilly had insisted on getting Jameli a puppy named Sammy, who dutifully trailed behind Jameli wherever she went.

Brandon had thrown himself into his work and church, which both turned out to be saviors. In the night, he cried his tears, cursed

God, repented and accepted that God's will be done. His financial status was more than solid as he dutifully worked with his father's investment advisor over the years and was already poised for early retirement, should he choose it.

Because he taught by choice not necessity, he was free to focus on giving his best to the students. His efforts brought him in at second place for best teacher in the county last year. This year, he was in the lead to be number one with the additions of the young men's transition program and his coaching the JV soccer girl's championship team.

Yet for all the positive things happening in his life to distract him from his past, seeing a full-grown Dr. Altha Harkens made the greatest impact. She was a stunning beauty with an infectious smile. She was intelligent and still had some pushback in her that made her earn his respect. But unlike the freshman he met all those years ago, there was a mature understanding of life in her eyes. He wasn't sure if it was the loss of her father, or seeing so much pain in the field of medicine, but there was more giving in her than he remembered.

It was fun spending time with and talking to her. To think he was assisting with a medical mystery was incredible. Although the topic was hitting close to home, he admired her efforts to find out more about what was protecting the pregnant women in her community. He enjoyed meeting Uncle Lou out of a church setting and smiled at the old man's comments about them being a handsome couple that would have beautiful babies. One day, Brandon would have to thank the man for his help.

It had been years since the idea of being with a woman crossed his mind. In the presence of a full-grown Altha, a sensual spark flared in him. He didn't know if it was her lean, toned body, her height, flawless skin, or her smile, but whatever it was, it moved him towards life. When they were in the forest sanctuary by the spring, toasting "to healing," there was a secret intimacy about the act.

Her movements were graceful as she dipped for him first to share the spring water. When she bent over, Brandon took in her shapely figure gasped and then blushed as a long dormant warmth began rising from deep inside his center. Only after he was served did she get her own cup of water and in doing so, displayed an unselfish spirit. During their toast to healing, he lost himself in her dark, beautiful eyes and that earlier small spark flared into a small fire.

It was when he returned alone to the spring to fill the gallon jug of water to share with Aunt Lilly, that the natural beauty of the scene took a turn towards the supernatural. Brandon followed the path and as he entered the woods, he was again overcome with a sense of peace and serenity. In the alcove of the spring, he bent down to dip the jug and while it was filling, an unexpected pleasant breeze flowed through the trees.

He heard the words whispered as clear as day, "It is well!" As soon as he finished filling the jug, he turned around, expecting to see Altha, but found himself alone. As he scanned the woods, there was no one to be found—only a pair of mourning doves, fluttering in an opening and cooing over the babble of the spring.

Brandon knew he had distinctly heard the words, "It is well!" But what was more confounding was they were said in Swahili, "Ni vizuri." Looking farther into the woods, he was puzzled as again, he saw no Altha and no other human being. He didn't tremble in fear as the whispered declaration held universal understanding and was of comfort. He was perplexed and didn't know what to make of the experience as he walked up the trail to leave the woods.

Brandon was deep in thought when he lifted his eyes and saw Altha moving gracefully through Uncle Lou's plush garden of pastel flowers. The bright flowers and blossoms outlined her form as her dark, shimmering skin and brilliant smile seemed to outshine them all. The breathtaking scene reminded him of the art piece they had first bonded over all those years ago.

It was at that moment that his small brewing fire for Altha flashed into a firestorm that could only be quenched by her. Brandon was speechless over the whispered words he heard by the spring and by what he saw anew in Altha in the gardens. He was silent and thinking of his next move as he walked with her to the car.

When he dropped her off at Starbucks, before she could pull off, he exited his car and jogged over and reached in to shake her hand to thank her for letting him be her partner again. What would she think if she knew he was shaking her hand in order to simply touch her again? He needed reassurance that the burning he felt start in his core, travel up his back, to settle on his chest and make his heart skip a beat was a real feeling.

It first happened Tuesday evening in her front yard when they met after all these years. He truly felt something again earlier in the day when they shook hands at Starbucks. He prayed she didn't think he was crazy or weird by shaking her hand that last time. While Brandon didn't know exactly what was going on in him, he knew he liked it.

   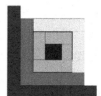

CHAPTER 12

✳ ✳ ✳

THAT SIMPLE

I t was Thursday morning, and after three nights of being at home, Altha felt refreshed. It was good to know she wouldn't have to return to work until Monday of the following week. She was thankful for her decision to leave for Dublin and Tee's baby shower weekend early. As she helped with morning chores, she tried to think about the mystery of the medical safety zone, but her thoughts were interrupted by images of Brandon, and Uncle Lou's words, "handsome couple."

Coming from the barn, she stopped for a second to look closer at one of the numerous pear trees in their small orchard. It was white and in full bloom. The blossoms were under attack by hundreds of bees. As the bees entered the blooms, the entire branch began to arch and shake and with it, a small number of petals gently fell to the ground. Seeing Zora Neal Hurston's description of natural love firsthand, Altha could understand why even Zora might get a little hot and bothered watching nature in action.

She had to admit that since meeting Brandon, a long dormant part of her had been awakened. As a physician, she had mastered the ability to compartmentalize her emotions in order to keep calm in a crisis. With Brandon, it seemed that a part of her authentic self had been stirred. He stimulated that common thread that was woven into each part of her person; a thread that ran across all of her superficial, professional boundaries, but was anchored to her personal core. Something happened to her when she was near Brandon. She felt like spring.

Her mother interrupted her daydreaming to have her take a pound cake over to Mrs. Evelynn's. When she arrived, her godmother welcomed her in, and guided Altha to set the cake on a serving table. Knowing without her asking that Mrs. Evelynn would need her to help set up the tables, Altha pulled them from the storage closet. She dutifully set up the tables then chairs.

Mrs. Evelynn helped her put on the tablecloths, placemats, napkins, silverware and centerpieces. Altha stopped to look at one of Mrs. Evelynn's older family pictures that showed a smiling, younger and thinner Mrs. Evelynn with her husband who had passed away. She wondered if she would ever find that type of happiness. She didn't notice Mrs. Evelynn approaching her.

"What's on your mind?" Mrs. Evelynn asked. "I hope you're not going crazy."

Both women laughed. Altha said, "No, I keep telling you I'm not going crazy. I'm just...frustrated." She went on to share that Mrs. Evelynn and her mom were right about there not being many deaths during pregnancy around Dublin. "I've been trying to figure out why and I can't. It's not slavery, haints, the spring water or the birthing ring tradition. I don't know what it is."

Before she could continue, Mrs. Evelynn interrupted her. "It's the quilt, dummy."

Altha frowned. "The quilt? What do you mean? How?"

Mrs. Evelynn said, "Stella started the tradition of the quilting. I can start off on the story, but its best to talk to Aunt Flossie, because she is Stella's granddaughter. What I know is, around here, when a woman becomes pregnant, her family and friends start a quilt. The first piece of cloth is always done by Aunt Flossie. Before that, her mother Vivian would start it, and before that, it was Stella herself. Once started, women who are friends, church members, family and sometimes enemies help to build the quilt. Half is done before the baby comes and half is done after the baby's here. It usually takes about five or six weeks after the birthing for the quilt to be finished. The last piece of quilt is done by Aunt Flossie as well. All the men at church and in the community know this fact."

Mrs. Evelynn leaned close and whispered. "Until the quilt is finished, the couple can't start their love relations. She grinned. "So if you see young men acting extra nice to Aunt Flossie, that's why."

Altha thought of her quilt in her apartment in Atlanta. Quilts were a natural part of her daily life growing up. Like old chairs, there were old pillows and old quilts around. When Altha was a girl, she helped with countless quilts. Aunt Flossie herself helped to guide and teach Altha's small hands to sew. She remembered the easy Rocking stitch and the Tie stitch and the more complicated Loading the needle stitch. Each one Aunt Flossie taught her, she had dutifully mastered.

Altha, as the oldest girl, would accompany her mother to the sewing circles where gossip, church talk, love talk, and family talk ruled. She kept attending them until the age of fourteen, when she started high school and knew she wanted to go into the sciences. The idea of becoming a doctor, although a distant dream at that time, had filled her thoughts.

Before Altha could ask a follow-up question, her phone rang. When she answered, it was her mother speaking with joyful excitement. "Tee's going into labor. I'm about to be a grandmother and you are about to be an auntie!"

Altha said her thanks and goodbyes to Mrs. Evelynn, then headed straight over to the house to pick up her mother and take her to the hospital.

The birthing was flawless, and James and Tee worked as a team. There was no drama, only the palpable love James had for Tee, and a tenderness she had for James as they welcomed Josiah, a beautiful son, into the family and the world. Josiah burst on the scene at 4:30 pm on Thursday. After seeing her new nephew, Altha let Tee get some rest and promised to return later that night to relieve her mother who was sitting with Tee.

Altha needed to make a special stop before going back to the hospital. As she drove, she looked at the clouds that would make up the day's sunset and recalled what her mother preached about silver linings. Altha knew if it had not been for the trauma of her past weekend at work, she would not have been present for the birth of her first nephew or able to support her mother. God worked it out and she prayed He had a little more mercy to help her with one other small miracle.

She completed her errand and returned to the hospital. When she entered her room, Tee was finishing a feeding and extended her arms to hand Josiah to his only aunt. Earlier, each of his uncles called, one after the other, to Facetime, see the new family member and check on their little sister. In this moment, there was only love in the room. All was good with the world.

As Altha held Josiah and memorized his every feature and smelled his new baby scent, Tee spoke softly, "You know there's no reason you can't have a baby of your own."

Altha smirked, but before she could give a negative response, Tee said, "I know you think you know everything, and that we argue like cats and dogs, but we argue because you don't listen to me."

She continued with heartfelt sincerity, "It's like you already think you know what I'm going to say and have committed to how you think. I don't know why, but I have to say things three different ways for you to truly hear me once. It can be so frustrating not being heard."

Altha was surprised by her sister's candor.

Tee finished her comments with a declaration and challenge. "In order for me to do right by this child, you and I need to be on good terms." With a penetrating wisdom that Altha couldn't deny, she said "Great families raise great children."

The room was silent except for Josiah's cooing. Altha wasn't swimming with a shark. She was in the water with someone who had expressed true concern for her and seemed to be sending her a lifeline. She helped raise Tee, but was gone as Tee grew into this phenomenal woman. Was she still approaching Tee as if she were that fifteen-year-old rebel? Had she ever given a thought to the fact that people grow and mature and learn? Had being away and her high-end training lowered the position of her only sister in her thoughts?

Looking out into the night, seeing the reflection of herself holding Josiah in the window, Altha admitted that at times with her siblings, she could be authoritarian and a know-it-all. Maybe as her career and schooling advanced, it made her even more of an expert on everything and unwilling to listen to other opinions. Had this created the gulf that developed between the two sisters? At that moment, it was crystal clear that Altha had been in the wrong, but she had a remedy that might work.

She turned to her younger yet mature sister, nodded and looking at Josiah, straightened her shoulders, lifted her chin, looked Tee straight in the eyes and said, "I'm sorry."

As the tears began to flow, she said, "I love you with all my heart and I'm so proud of who you've become. You've grown into a strong woman, wife, and mother and it's beautiful to see."

Handing Josiah back to Tee, Altha went to her tote bag and pulled out two cups and a Thermos filled with the healing spring water. Her errand had been to get the water, hoping it would heal her relationship with her sister. She filled their two cups and handed one to Tee. Altha lifted hers towards Tee and said, "To healing "and with the intonation of a prayer over her younger sister declared "Kuponya"

Tee lifted her cup and responded with a warm smile, "To healing." As her big sister coached her in pronouncing the foreign Swahili Tee repeated with reverence "Kuponya."

Eyes interlocked as they finished their cups with one lift. The sisters hugged with the new boy child in between, and a family bond that had been strained was restored through the resiliency sprung from centuries of mutual support, sacrifice, and love.

They fellowshipped and laughed and talked for a while. Tee put Josiah in the basinet. They wiped their tears and hugged again as Altha began collecting her things to prepare to head home. Before she could turn, Tee grasped her hand.

"I'm serious about you having a baby of your own."

Altha moved closer to Tee on the bed. "Little Sis, can I tell you that I don't even know how to get started in a relationship? My head was in a book for almost nine years. To be honest, with all that studying, I had no social life."

Tee smiled. "I can teach you a few things if you're willing to listen."

Altha looked up to the ceiling and let out a deep breath of exasperation.

Tee grabbed her hands and squeezed them. "Get ready. I'm about to give you a sister-to-sister lesson on love. Lesson number one—with the next brother you're interested in, take the time to listen to him closely and hear him in earnest. Identify what he needs to be his best self—not what he wants—then unselfishly provide for that need, not expecting anything in return."

Tee paused a minute to let that sink in. She finished by saying, "It's that simple."

Altha raised a brow. "It's that simple?"

Tee squeezed her hands again. "It's that simple."

James entered the room and looked surprised at the emotional scene he interrupted. He looked even more surprised when Altha stood and gave him a warm hug. She whispered to him, "Thank you for loving my baby sister."

✳ ✳ ✳

Early Friday morning, Altha joined a crew of women at James and

Tee's house to help complete Josiah's nursery. Working with her mom and James's mom, the women made short work of Josiah's new digs. Tee and the baby would be home Saturday morning, and they wanted things perfect. Annabelle and James's mother agreed to split the household duties, helping Tee during the first week. The two new grandmothers had been friends for years before their children found each other. Altha had forgotten the blessings that can accompany lifelong friendships.

When they finished at noon, Altha received a text from Brandon congratulating her on being a new aunt. He asked if she was available to come to Mrs. Baker's for some dinner. Although she was tired from the excitement of the new baby and setting up the nursery, she agreed to come by at 6 pm.

Mrs. Baker lived five miles from the Harkens homestead on a quiet road in a single-level, brick house. After Altha pulled to a stop, Jameli greeted her, holding an energetic puppy. She took her by the hand and the two walked into the house.

The table was already set with cold glasses of spring water. Mrs. Baker and Jameli laid out a classic soul food dinner with greens, yams, and baked chicken. Dessert was a decadent peach cobbler and Brandon's personally prepared cups of Kenyan Kericho Gold chai tea mixed with ginger and milk. The food and company were welcoming. Altha fit right in with the three. Altha and Brandon handled the dishes after the meal, then they all went onto the back porch to enjoy the chai tea.

Sitting in rockers, they began to talk and covered a broad set of topics from politics to international health, education, and HBCU's versus predominantly White colleges. Their conversation was light and filled with laughter. Altha listened to more about Brandon's travels in Kenya and Mrs. Baker chimed in about her visit to Kenya to participate in Brandon's wedding. She excitedly described how weddings there were more than just between the bride and groom, but were a joining of families.

The laughs were loudest when Mrs. Baker described how, on

the fly, she had to learn how to pick out the good cows from the bad ones as she and their family sponsor, Mr. Rono prepared a proper dowry.

Altha was amazed as she described the steps involved in the courtship and the wedding. The two families meet and before any transactions are discussed, the bride-to-be publicly declares for all to hear, "I have chosen this man." Her vivid recounting of the beauty of the country and the ceremonies captured Altha.

Jameli added to Mrs. Baker's descriptions as they painted a picture of a wonderful people and land. Sipping her tea, Altha could see the images they were creating and a longing to visit Kenya stirred in her.

That night, Jameli made Altha promise to come to her soccer game the next afternoon. Altha agreed to come if Jameli, Mrs. Baker and Brandon would come over for Sunday brunch before she left for Atlanta. With everyone in agreement, Jameli asked Altha to tuck her into bed for the night. Altha knelt next to Jameli for her bedtime prayers. Her heart was warmed when the child included her in her blessings. With Jameli and Mrs. Baker both retired for the night, Brandon and Altha went back onto the porch.

The night was warm and scents of flowers in full bloom were on a subtle breeze that enveloped the two. When Brandon asked about the mystery of the medical safety zone, she admitted that the arrival of Josiah put things on hold, but according to Mrs. Evelynn, it was the quilt. She shared everything Mrs. Evelynn had told her.

"I'll go visit Aunt Flossie to finalize the information, but for now, it's all about my new nephew. I'm looking forward to learning more about Miss Stella. She certainly knew her people and the importance of traditions."

Altha yawned. The day's activities had caught up to her and she needed to go home and rest. Brandon walked her to her car.

"I can't believe how time has passed. I'll be heading back to Atlanta on Sunday night." For a moment, she thought she saw a fleeting expression of hurt cross Brandon's face that pained her heart.

The look passed and he said, "You should come back home more often."

The moonlight shone down on them. Altha waited for his next words to fill the silence. Instead, having arrived at the car, he extended his hand, shook hers warmly and said good night.

Altha entered her car and sat for a few moments, watching Brandon casually walk away. She whispered to herself, "There goes that handshake again."

He was a perfect gentleman, but for a moment, standing with him enveloped in the warm Georgia night laced with the scents of spring flowers, she wished he hadn't been. In the dark, her eyes couldn't share with him the yearning in her bosom for his touch. He was too far from her to feel the heat rising from her insides, flushing her cheeks, sweating her brow, and moistening her lips as if they were preparing for another bite of peach cobbler.

His hands were strong and soft, and his actions were tentative. She knew he had loved before and been hurt, and she respected his need for a time out. But Lord, she wanted to get him off the bench and into the game.

Driving home slowly, she tried to remind herself of what Tee said.

What does Brandon need? She repeated it over and over again, committing to stepping out on faith and earning Brandon's favor if ever given a chance. It was at these times that she wished she were the precocious, extroverted Tee. But she had listened to Tee's Lesson Number One and promised herself to act.

Two steps after Brandon turned to head back to the house, the warmth from Altha's touch had already traveled to his chest. He mused that she was worth a herd of cattle and a flock of sheep. The night obscured the full smile that graced his face as he walked on in deep thought, knowing for sure there was something about Altha that moved him. In his younger days, under that mystic moonlight, he would have coaxed her into his arms and tried to kiss her full, beautiful lips.

But he was older now and wiser. Having been in love and having lost, he knew the real thing when he saw it. Pursuing Neema taught him the importance of patience and taking time to make the proper, solid steps when a man is serious about a woman. He earned Neema's hand and the respect of her family and would do the same with Altha's. He recognized her value and his intentional approach and thoughtfulness would be rewarded ten times over if he achieved her affections.

Brandon savored the slow intensity of the new feelings Altha brought forth in him. He didn't want to take the chance of injuring a future between them by going too fast. Deep in his spirit, he had chosen her, but he was not clear that she would choose him. Yet sure as a morning sunrise brings forth a new song in the two doves that nested outside his window, he knew his path to happiness led straight to the arms of Dr. Altha Harkens.

He got to the house and opened the door. There was no question he would have a restless night, quelling his mental, spiritual, and physical desires for the once understated freshman beauty who was now an overpoweringly beautiful, sensual woman.

   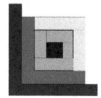

CHAPTER 13

✳ ✳ ✳

HIS ART AFICIONADO

Saturday morning, Altha arose refreshed, and before opening her eyes, listened to a pair of cardinals eagerly greeting the day. Her day would be full. In the morning, she would take her mother to Tee's house to welcome Josiah home. At noon, she would go over to Mrs. Evelynn's to put away those card tables from Thursday's bridge game , and she would close out her day by going to Jameli's soccer game.

Everything was going well for mother and child as Altha, her mother, and James' mother welcomed Tee home and got Josiah situ-ated in his new nursery. Tee's face was beaming with appreciation and thanks. James looked on with pride as his wife and son were pampered. By noon, Altha left to make her way over to Mrs. Evelynn's.

When she entered Mrs. Evelynn's home, Altha put the tables up before joining her godmother for lunch at the kitchen table. A quilt was draped over one of the chairs and after clearing the plates, Mrs. Evelynn unfolded it and began running her aged hands over it. The quilt brought a smile to her face as the memories it possessed be-gan to rise. This quilt was made for her first child, Kathleen, and the design. It touched it with the others as she pointed out Aunt Flossie's start-off piece of cloth.

its intricacy and depth of detail. She was reminded of her needing to visit Aunt Flossie before she left. Altha was patient as Mrs. Evelynn pointed out the pieces Aunt Flossie had placed and Altha recognized her mother's unique patterned stitching that was almost as unique as her mother's handwriting. There were five rows of ten individual cloth patches of all colors, but united, they created a masterpiece that had kept Mrs. Evelynn's family warm over the years.

Mrs. Evelynn reached into her pocket to bring out an old, wooden, carved ring. As she shared it with Altha, it was easy to recognize Uncle Lou's workmanship. The ring was maple colored and worn. Mrs. Evelynn smiled warmly and reached over to share the keepsake with Altha. As Altha held the ring, she wondered if she would ever need to use the one she received from Uncle Lou.

It was 4:30 when Altha turned into Dublin's new soccer complex. It was a perfect day for an afternoon game. The crowd was filled with siblings and parents encouraging the two girls' teams. She joined Brandon who was holding Jameli's puppy in the stands, and cheering Jameli's efforts. They made small talk in between the game's action, and she caught herself a few times admiring Brandon's profile. They cheered together and Jameli waved at them from the playing field.

After the game, as the crowd thinned out, Brandon was standing alone next to the end of the stands taking in the beautiful sunset. He was watching Jameli alone on the field, in the setting rays, playing with her puppy. Altha, remembering Tee's instructions, knew it was her time to move. Approaching Brandon from behind, she stood on the first row of the bleachers, put her hands on his waist, and placed her chin on his shoulder, as if she had done it a thousand times in the past. Then she began to speak.

Her instructions were clear and firm, but tender. "Look into the sunset and see what I see." She used his own familiar words he had whispered into her ear long ago. She pointed out the blazing colors of the sunset that served as a background for his daughter joyfully playing. Then she described his positive effects on the community, reminding him of avenues where he could do good.

"You brought healing with you from across the sea that is helping young men to grow here. Remember how the town welcomed you with open arms, returning your energy in kind."

She pointed at Jameli. "See how her smooth, flawless skin is an eternal beauty and an everlasting representation of the joy of her mother and the love of her father. That wondrous child is poised to do great things that will change the world. Your daughter's presence places a salving potion over you daily that through Christ, will heal all hurts."

✳ ✳ ✳

Brandon was startled by Altha's touch, not having had anyone in his personal space in years. He felt the warmth of her closeness and her breasts on his back. She felt like a burden his body was designed to carry and he wanted to defend her from the world. He exhaled and relaxed, stepping back to lean more into her arms, knowing there was no denying she fit him.

As Altha spoke, her words caressed his ears and moved his spirit. When she said, "See what I see," her lips slightly touched his ears, sending shock waves down his spine. For the first time in two years, he completely let his guard down and knew with certainty, he and Jameli would be all right.

To the uninformed observer, it looked as if Altha were simply pointing out the dimensions of the park and playing field, but in reality, she was sharing with Brandon a new view of his life's potential. Brandon's last memory before a full out-of-body experience was Altha tenderly kissing his ear which catapulted him into ecstasy, and in an instant, made his whole world brighter.

He was watching a new, more vibrant sunset lost in the novelty of its beauty when he internalized the message of this God-given, living piece of art. The scene spoke to him with the unmistakable message that life was for the living and he should live! Live! Live! Until his last breath.

He knew life and the world were calling him to get back fully into living. He recalled the whispered words, "*Ni vizuri*—It is well," and knew God's grace would cover the spirits of his loved ones lost.

The emotional insight made his eyes begin to water which broke nature's spell. It was only when a tear fell from his eye, warming his cheek that he realized he was standing in thought alone. He turned to look for the missing piece in his life. Where was Altha?

His eyes found her easily. She had her arms crossed and was leaning against a blooming dogwood tree watching over both him and Jameli. Her first words made him laugh. She pointed at herself and said, "I am the Art…"

Brandon nodded and conceded she had captured his heart and taken him to a better place before he whispered in newfound love, "Aficionado."

Brandon slowly approached Altha and gently took her into his arms and the two shared a full body hug. He whispered, "Thank you for giving me what I needed."

The words settled between the two and the heat from the touching of their bodies began to grow. Brandon savored the moment, feeling as if his best self was being resurrected. Near Altha, he had begun to dream again. He wanted her and he could see by the look in her eyes that she wanted him too.

Before they could go further, Altha received a call from her mother. He watched her face go from a broad smile to one of panic. "Okay, I'm coming."

She looked up at him. "Tee isn't feeling well and is having some unexpected bleeding. I need to go take my mom to the hospital."

CHAPTER 14

✳ ✳ ✳

The Strength In Our Common Thread

Altha immediately switched into doctor mode. Her disposition became calm, and she felt herself falling into her professional persona of the no nonsense, compartmentalized clinician. After breaking away from Brandon, she started towards her car. But after one step, she turned and instinctively ran over to Jameli, bent down, and gave the child a warm hug that Jameli returned in full. Only then did Altha sprint to her car.

On the way to the hospital, Altha wondered what the problem was. She shuddered as an image of the blood on her scrubs and shoes after her last case at the hospital flashed into her mind. Knowing 60% of pregnancy-related deaths occurred after the child was delivered, she ran the list of possible problems.

Tee didn't have blood pressure problems during the pregnancy, and after the pregnancy, she had still looked good with no swelling of the face and hands. Eclampsia—uncontrolled high blood pressure and other deadly symptoms would have been the worst thing because it could cause kidney failure, heart failure, strokes and seizures.

She hoped it wasn't like Serena Williams' case where a blood clot formed and moved to her lungs. If a blood clot was identified late, it was tough to deal with and could be catastrophic. As Altha neared the hospital, she readied herself to enter a storm of confusion and a battle to help her little sister as best she could.

At the front desk, Altha was directed to the waiting room. Walking with urgency, she entered the door of the waiting room and froze mid-step. There in the room were over twenty Black women of all ages quietly standing. Silent and respectful, their impact was overwhelming. She saw Mrs. Baker, Olivia – Tee's best friend from middle school, Jeannette Ross, her mother and numerous others who she had seen or heard dropped by the house to bring a gift and help with Tee's quilt.

Mrs. Evelynn's words, "It's the quilt, dummy "echoed into her memory, as she heard Mrs. Evelynn enter behind her, announcing her presence to the waiting room.

Altha was overwhelmed by the love and support of this women's community for her little sister. Much as she wanted to greet and hug every woman and express her appreciation, she needed to talk to the doctor to see what was going on. She wandered down the hall in search of the emergency room doctor that had seen Tee when she came in.

She walked up just in time to overhear a conversation between the young ER doc that James pointed out and the gray-haired, more experienced Dr. Harris that Altha knew from her childhood in Dublin. Neither of them seemed to see her standing there as they discussed Tee's case. Altha decided to take advantage of that fact and see what she could find out without them perhaps keeping information from her, knowing she was a physician.

Dr. Ellis looked quite young. Altha didn't think he could be more than two years out of his residency training. She hoped he knew what he was doing. She stopped herself. She was just two years out of her anesthesia training and was very confident in her skills.

Dr. Ellis said, "There's a young patient I just saw in the ER that's two days post-partum that came in with some pain and bleeding. She looks fine and all her vital signs are stable. I think I'll give her some Motrin, send her home, and have her follow up on Monday."

Dr. Harris chuckled, the wisdom of his years in medicine summed up in a simple, "Hmmmm...."

"What? You don't agree?"

Dr. Harris stroked his white goatee. "Try that approach and see what happens. Come back and tell me how that goes for you."

Altha was perplexed by the conversation and wondered what Dr. Harris knew that Dr. Ellis didn't. Instead of approaching the two of them, she followed Dr. Ellis as he turned toward the waiting room.

When he entered, he stopped abruptly. He drew in a breath when he saw the twenty Black women gathered in the waiting room. James stood and came to shake his hand. He was in his police uniform.

Dr. Ellis greeted many of the women. Dublin was a small town so he probably knew many of them from the community.

James asked, "How's my wife?"

All the women in the room leaned in to hear the doctor's answer. Dr. Ellis appeared to draw back, as if he was overwhelmed that all the women were listening so intently.

"Ummm...she appears to be fine. Her vital signs are stable and her pain has reduced. I think we're going to..." his words trailed off as he looked around the room. "I think we're going to observe her overnight. We'll give her some IV fluids and I'll have the gynecologist on call to come and have a look at her."

Dr. Ellis went back down the hall with Altha following close, but not too close behind. Dr. Harris was waiting for him at the nurse's station with a big grin on his face.

Dr. Ellis smiled. "You knew didn't you?"

Dr. Harris patted the young doctor on the back in a fatherly way. "Don't worry. The first time it happens, it's a bit of a shock. In these parts, women look after each other. I'm sure you probably decided to admit the lady and watch her overnight. It wouldn't be a bad idea to have the gynecologist on call come in to make sure everything's okay."

Dr. Ellis laughed. "That's exactly what I decided to do. Wow...I guess you've been in this community for a while. You know these women well."

Dr. Harris nodded. "If it's any consolation, those women usually show up when something's going on with a patient. They seem to sense it." Dr. Harris concluded. "You're doing the right thing." He gave him a reassuring nod and walked off.

Altha slowly walked back toward the waiting room, thinking about what she had just witnessed. She now knew it was indeed the quilt that was adding protection for the women of Dublin surrounding childbirth. She knew all the more that she hadn't gotten the whole story from Mrs. Evelynn and that the visit to Aunt Flossie that she promised to make the first day of her arrival would be the key to helping her understand the full story. Provided Tee was okay tonight, she was headed to spend some time with her old quilting coach, Aunt Flossie.

Altha joined James and her mother, discussed the plan and agreed that it was best. Tee saw the gynecologist within the hour, and it was thought some small parts of the placenta might still be in her that needed to be removed. The procedure was short. By 8:00 pm, Tee was out of the operating room. She was placed on some antibiotics and was to be watched closely for infection overnight and provided all went well, would be sent home the next day.

Altha stayed until Tee was safely out of the operating room and resting on the obstetrics ward. The other women departed as soon as the decision to raise the level of Tee's care was made, and when Annabelle agreed her daughter was getting the best attention. Annabelle would stay part of the night with Tee. Altha left heading straight to Aunt Flossie's.

   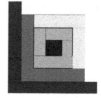

CHAPTER 15

✳ ✳ ✳

STELLA

It was after dark when Altha reached Aunt Flossie's house. Her thoughts were spinning with the realization that she had solved the medical mystery. Her community, through tradition and foresight, created a medical safety zone for its women during their most vulnerable time. It was late and the day had been long, but her questions would not wait until the next morning.

She smiled to herself at the ingenuity of using the tradition of quilting to build a healthcare safety net. Her overall feeling was gratitude. She was thankful for where she was raised, thankful for her family and thankful for the strength of the sisterhood displayed at the hospital that evening.

The porch light was on at Aunt Flossie's house, a modern construction built on land that had been in her family for generations. The home was outlined by the shadows of two large, ancient, oak trees. Altha knew the yard well. As a child, she ate the figs, plums, peaches and apples from the trees as she assisted Aunt Flossie. Elderberry bushes and an herb garden were always active at the home, along with a beehive for Aunt Flossie's natural honey.

As if on cue, as Altha opened the outer porch screen door, Aunt Flossie opened her front door. The look on the face of the short, full-figured, grey-haired woman dressed in a house coat said it all. She had been expecting Altha.

Without speaking, she ushered Altha in out of the darkness and into an inviting foyer and living room. The faces of Aunt Flossie's family on the photos that lined the hall seemed to smile as Altha entered and was guided to a couch. In front of her on an antique coffee table were two family photo albums and a maroon velvet cloth satchel with the outline of a book it held.

Aunt Flossie had a sweet grin on her face. "Why Altha, I had a feeling you would be dropping by. Mrs. Evelynn told me about Tee and that you had some questions about quilting. I know you know how to quilt since I'm the one who taught you, but feels like you have deeper questions about quilting."

Altha remembered Aunt Flossie guiding her hands as a child, then as a youth, showing her the stitches.

Aunt Flossie said, "God is good. You were a wonderful young quiltmaker and back in the day, we would have had you become a midwife. But we are so proud you became a doctor."

Altha replied, "You taught me how to quilt, Aunt Flossie. Now I'm old enough to understand why we quilt."

Aunt Flossie smiled and said, "Yes, you are. I'll pour the tea I heated for you." She disappeared into the kitchen.

Altha called out to her, "Your grandmother Stella sure started some serious traditions around here that are still helping out to this day. She must have been special."

Aunt Flossie called out, "Very special. That's her in the big picture in the middle."

Altha walked over to the wall of pictures and viewed a young woman with her hair up wearing a white lace dress that went up to her chin.

Aunt Flossie entered with teacups on a tray and a steaming teapot. Setting them on a table, she joined Altha at the picture wall.

She directed Altha's eyes to a family picture from around 1910 and began.

"Altha, allow me to introduce a woman who would be exceptional in any age—a true renaissance woman, my grandmother, Stella."

There were old, black-and-white pictures that had been partially restored decorating the walls. They showed Stella at various ages—as a young woman, a young wife with her husband, and as a mother with her husband and daughters, one of which was Aunt Flossie Mae's mother, Vivian.

When they moved to sit side by side on the couch, Aunt Flossie pointed out the two photo albums, one dedicated to Stella and the other showing the women of the different quilting sessions since the tradition began. The soft satchel held a small book filled with Stella's personal midwife lessons and teaching pearls she learned over the course of her career. Altha's introduction to Stella became more intimate as they opened the first picture book showing the young, beautiful and intelligent Stella.

It opened with a childhood school picture of a single-room elementary school, a single instructor and a group of children, Stella included. Another picture showed the old, wooden Dublin hospital with the full staff and Stella standing in the back row far left as if included as an afterthought. Other images showed Stella, her husband and three young girls.

Altha was drawn to a single picture of Stella standing alone in a white midwife dress and apron. Her expressions were mature and serious. She saw Stella's greying temples and another picture of her being presented an award by the mayor of Dublin. Finally, there were pictures of Stella in her old age, holding a brown-skinned girl child, Flossie, whose smile was just like hers. The obituary for Stella, who passed in 1973 at the age of eighty-two, mentioned her role as one of the last working midwives in the county.

Having introduced Stella's full life cycle, Aunt Flossie, Stella's grandchild, shared the tale of the fateful day that sparked the quilting tradition. As Stella told her daughter, Vivian, and Vivian told her daughter Flossie Mae, now Aunt Flossie shared with Altha, "It was all based on a matter of simple mathematics."

At the age of fourteen, Stella was guided into midwifery by the family elders and healers. She displayed the desire to learn how to heal and help people. As a child, she showed interest in nature and spent time quietly watching local healers and midwives until she was invited to see and understand more about God's gift of life. Although Stella had limited formal education, going only up to the eighth grade, she was a quick learner. She apprenticed under the watchful eye of her Aunt Sarah, the midwife who delivered Stella and her other siblings.

Aunt Sarah poured her decades of knowledge into her receiving student. Her aunt guided Stella's hands during Stella's first deliveries and showed her acceptable aftercare of the new mothers. Aunt Sarah noted Stella was different from the outset. Stella's eighth grade education meant she could read and learn from other sources than just her aunt. The youth was a voracious reader and an aggressive learner and after exhausting Aunt Sarah's and her network of friend's knowledge, at the age of seventeen, she obtained a job cleaning in the small women's ward in the Dublin hospital. For two years, she assisted in cleaning the all-White hospital, spending as much time as possible around the birthing rooms.

As an invisible janitor, she listened, learned and with the help of an old medical dictionary, read any information on health she could get. One day, she found an article in the trash where doctors were touting how magnesium sulfate could prevent the seizures from eclampsia. The symptoms describing eclampsia in the article were the spitting image of the "death shakes," the worst thing a midwife could deal with in a pregnant woman. Prayer, a quiet place and rest were the only treatments in the Black community and often, the outcomes were grave. The course without any treatment was well known and Stella had seen it during her apprenticeship.

The symptoms were swelling hands and face and then a bad

headache not relieved by aspirin, stomach pains, then shortness of breath, whole body shaking then seizures and death in its worst cases. While the focus was the mothers, at best, six in ten of the babies died if the mothers developed the seizures. According to the article, magnesium sulfate was a possible treatment.

While performing cleaning tasks, Stella listened to the doctors talking about how some of the white women were being treated with the magnesium and survived the "death shakes." The word "magnesium," struck a chord with the young Stella. She had seen an article in the *Saturday Evening Post* on the importance of diet and nutrition. In an old general health book, vitamins and nutrients were mentioned and home remedies for everything from dropsy to bowel issues were included.

The eighteen-year-old Stella thought, if magnesium sulfate was the cure being given to the white women on the birthing ward, how could she get some for the pregnant Black women she was taking care of? As usual, she was thinking in a way few of her peers would understand. She was not thinking in limitations, but like all mathematicians, began by using what was given to solve a problem.

Stella kept reading anything she could get her hands on, wherever she could get her hands on it. One day, she was emptying a trash can and found a newspaper in it. She stopped cleaning and quickly browsed to see if there was anything of interest in the paper. She froze when she felt eyes on her. She looked up and saw Nurse Anne, a white nurse in the hospital who appeared to be only a few years older than her.

"Sorry, I was just..." Stella stopped. She couldn't think of an excuse to give.

Anne smiled warmly. "You were just doing what you always do. I always see you reading something." And she walked off.

Over her stay at the hospital, Stella and Nurse Anne never spoke of it again, but Stella began finding more recent newspapers and even old books on health in the trash. Daily she also felt a quiet respect coming from Nurse Anne, which she returned.

Stella secretly read nutritional magazines and knew that if she could find a way to get this magnesium sulfate into her ladies, she might have the same lifesaving results in the medical article. While she wasn't much at making elixirs, she believed God always provided natural solutions for problems that arose in His creations.

She dove into *Poor Richard's Almanac, The American Magazine, Good Housekeeping,* and *Scientific American Magazine* for diets high in magnesium. Ever the organizer, she made a list of foods high in the nutrient. On the list were vegetables like black beans, turnip greens, and lettuce and fruits like figs, blackberries, bananas, prunes and raisins. One day, her mentor, Aunt Sarah, mentioned in passing the answer she needed—Epsom salt baths.

It turns out Epsom salt is magnesium sulfate, and by taking a warm bath in Epsom salt, magnesium is taken in through the skin. With the new knowledge, Stella started her patients with early symptoms on a diet high in magnesium and a regimen of Epsom salt baths. To help with swelling, she turned to another natural remedy, nettle leaf tea, which made the mothers pee and lose fluid.

Fully vesting in natural healing, she planted some olive trees on her lot so as to have access to its mercurial extracts. She cultivated a year-round herb garden, and a honeybee hive added to her natural pharmacy. The first set of patients she managed as a midwife by herself were placed on the dietary changes.

Stella knew the strength of a midwife's place of influence in the village. Everyone listened to them because as the local health provider, each member of the community or their newborn's life at some time might depend on them. She knew her influence was growing in the community. Over the years, that influence began to grow and Stella was able to start two new traditions.

Knowing that a woman's hands swelling before or after delivery was an ominous sign of holding on to too much fluid, she started the first tradition of having her patients get birthing rings. The special rings would be worn from the first noting of pregnancy to six weeks after delivery. The rings identified pregnant women who were holding on to too much water, which might mean their kidneys or liver could be having problems, or at worst, could be the early signs of eclampsia – the death shakes.

The rings served another role as, after delivery, a woman needed time to heal and bond with her new child. When a mother removed her birthing ring, it was an indirect sign to her spouse that she was ready to return to normal love relations.

Stella added the second tradition of having the menfolk bring spring water to remind men to treat their wives special during the time they were carrying. She wanted and needed the special attention from her husband during all three of her pregnancies. It just so happened that the man who carved birthing rings for her patients had a natural spring on his property. A ring as a gift for the new mother-to-be, and a draw of spring water on a regular basis were enough to make any woman feel valued.

As a patient carried her child, if she had problems with her ring fitting too tight or needing to be cut off, Stella would hear about it through the grapevine and pay them a visit. Most of the time, a woman with swollen hands and face would immediately be placed on Stella's diet and would get medicine. The medicine was usually some form of aspirin which was almost the only medicine she had to work with. Epsom salt baths would be added and nettle tea as needed. Usually her approach worked, but sometimes, even she needed assistance.

It was 1930 and Stella was on the last two miles of a twelve-mile trip headed into Dublin. In those rural parts of Georgia, her mule and wagon were still more commonplace than automobiles. She was a thirty-eight-year-old Black woman traveling alone and had no fear of her neighbors, Black or White. She was one of the few Black faces welcomed into every home she was called to. As one of two midwives in the area, she had been called upon to assist to deliver hundreds of babies, both Black and White, over her twenty years in practice.

She was headed into town because two days before, she had

visited Haley Munford, a thirty-six-year-old who was having her fourth child. The first three had been hard on her and two of them were stillborn. Knowing her history, Stella checked in on her more often. She wasn't happy about what she saw. Haley was going to deliver sometime in the next two weeks and she had to remove her birthing ring because of swelling the same as she had during her third pregnancy when her child had passed away.

Stella started Haley on aspirin and the diet early and as far as she could tell, Haley was following instructions. When she saw her two days ago, Stella put some of Haley's pee in a shot glass. She placed a newspaper on the side of the glass and couldn't read the letters through the pee because it was cloudy, which was a bad sign. She threw the pee out the windows and checked where it fell after finishing three verses of the song, "Jesus Keep Me Near the Cross."

When she saw the numerous flies that were already drawn to the sweetness of the urine, Stella knew Haley had sugar and that the coming child would be larger and more difficult to handle than usual. Determined to avoid a stillborn and with Haley's ominous symptoms, Stella knew she needed some help.

As she entered town, she went to her old place of employment, the Dublin hospital, to the Black entrance, which was the back door of the small community hospital that served Whites only. They occasionally treated Blacks in dire distress. She asked for the same Nurse Anne she had worked for on the woman's ward in her younger days. Nurse Anne looked pleasantly surprised to see Stella and asked about her family and the children. Eventually, they got around to why Stella traveled into Dublin. Stella wanted to see the traveling doctor to ask a favor.

After a half hour wait, the young doctor came to the door and Stella politely told him about Haley Munford and asked if there were any way he might try to be in their area in the next week. The doctor said no, he was busy and then abruptly went back inside.

Stella sat for a minute, frustrated. She wasn't crushed. She had done right to follow her intuition and try to get every resource available to help Haley.

She didn't understand why the state seemed to be encouraging midwives to defer to young, inexperienced nurses and doctors. The writing was on the wall, but Stella felt she was one of the few who could read it. The midwives would be going away some day and the state health system, with its uncaring doctors and undertrained young nurses would be telling experienced, well-trained, Black midwives when and where they could deliver babies. Less home births by midwives and more hospital births with doctors and nurses was the future of medicine in Georgia.

She was about to get up into her wagon when she overheard a fateful discussion between the doctor and Nurse Anne.

Nurse Anne said, "Did you see Stella?"

"Yes." The doctor let out a flustered breath. "I won't be able to help her. I honestly didn't hear her well. My mind was on a patient in the hospital."

"She has a patient she's very concerned about. She's a very good midwife, so if she's concerned, I'm sure there's a problem. You should listen to her."

He scratched his head. "My wife always tells me I never listen to women. And especially Black women. It would take the words of ten Black women to get me to move as if I heard one White woman."

"In Stella's community, she's one of only two midwives that care for both Black and White patients. She's one of the first people called to help in other illnesses as well. So, if the voice of one White woman is needed to make sure that Stella is heard on this day, then hear my voice. Provide Stella with whatever she asks for."

Nurse Anne's voice was firm as she finished. "Stella is too proud of a person to ask for help if she doesn't need it. She must really need it. Please help her."

Stella smiled to herself, thinking of her silent relationship with Nurse Anne in the past. She was a caring healer and Stella appreciated her fighting for her and her patient.

Mounting the wagon, Stella turned her mule and started easing it back onto the road heading out of town. Before she could cross the road, she heard the young doctor shout out and jog from the front Whites only entrance of the hospital up to her wagon.

He looked her in the eyes and said with sincerity, "I heard you, Stella. I will make my best effort to be within striking distance one week from now."

Stella graciously thanked him and got her mule moving towards home. Even before she was out of town, she was working with the math equation. The voice of one White woman equals the voices of ten Black women. Stella wasn't surprised at the math as she had lived long enough to know her Black life and the lives of her community members weren't as valued by the people in charge of the resources. What was most surprising was that the doctor honestly admitted he could hear, but just couldn't quite hear Stella. She thought how difficult it must be to have a heart for doing good, but selective hearing that unevenly doled out one's services and lifesaving healing grace.

$1x=10y$…basic math.

The idea came that night after Stella finished sewing for her family.

The Given: Nurse Anne wouldn't be there forever to help her be heard. Stella knew she too would die someday and wouldn't always be there to protect her patients. Who would help the mothers when they were at their most vulnerable? Who would protect them and make sure they would be heard? Even the tradition of the early warning system using birthing rings she put in place would not help if there was no one to hear her patient's pleas. As Stella rubbed her hands on the quilt that kept her husband and family warm, that night the answer became crystal clear.

She would modify the tradition of making quilts. Her square would be the first and would tell the story for the midwives that would follow. Her starting patch would be fashioned from one of three, common, historical patterns that guided the Underground

Railroad, selected based on her knowledge of the mother's health history.

The jagged "X" shape of the drunkard's pattern meant danger—the mother was at higher than normal risk for problems. The triangular layered shapes of the flying geese pattern meant the mother was at low risk for problems. The North Star pattern was for all those in between the two extremes.

Drunkard's Path

Flying Geese

North Star

Log Cabin (Home Free)

Because the majority of women to have problems did so after delivery, she would assure half the women helped with the quilt before delivery and the other half came to help afterwards for about six weeks. The women from the community and church could choose when to lay their cloth squares down and during which time period they would commit to support the mother if she was in need.

Support for the new mother would come by quietly showing up at the house or hospital in case of a health issue to stand silently, and in doing so, make sure that the woman's voice was being heard. Stella would finish the quilt by placing the last patch, five or six weeks after the birth when the risk for problems was gone. The last patch would always be some form of the underground symbol for the log cabin, meaning home free. The birthing ring would then go back in the drawer until the mother was blessed to become with child again.

Altha could feel Aunt Flossie's enthusiasm. She was incredibly proud of her, Stella and their small community. For decades, there had been a community effort to protect and support its most vulnerable members. Stella was something special.

Altha eyed her community with new reverence. She was amazed the tradition had been holding and the women had been working together for nearly 100 years to support each other during childbirth.

Over the years, small changes in the tradition did occur. Instead of getting fresh drawn water from the healing spring each first day of the month, some of the men would keep a pitcher of it in the refrigerator. Also, when it came to birthing rings, some of the men, as men are bound to do, began competing on the quality and value of the birthing ring. Although Uncle Lou would have given them one for free, many now purchased birthing rings at a jeweler. The women still wore them from the time they were pregnant until the quilt was done, six weeks after delivery.

If swelling of the hands and fingers occurred with headaches, Aunt Flossie would know and encourage women to early care by a doctor. When they went, they would be accompanied by nearly twenty Black women, to assure that the mother was heard.

Aunt Flossie had altered how she laid down the starting piece of cloth for the quilt. On the chosen Underground symbol, she added a small diamond sewn in its top right corner. If the thread was green, the woman was dependable enough to seek help and speak up for herself. If it was red, then some, often unspoken event, had occurred in the woman's life that made it more difficult for her to speak up and verbally protect herself in the health system.

One out of every five quilts she made had a red diamond. These women had to be approached gently, and sometimes found it more difficult to bear being touched in private places. During pregnancy, they needed to be visited more and encouraged to express themselves. After they delivered, these same women would need more support and needed extra help to find their voices and engage in proper follow-up care.

Altha sat quietly overwhelmed by the history lesson. "Thanks, Aunt Flossie.

Flossie slowly but clearly said, "You know, Altha, I'm getting old."

Altha immediately knew what Aunt Flossie was asking by her comment. She paused and nodded. "Yes, I know."

She knew Aunt Flossie had chosen her as a child many years ago to plant seeds of service that were about to yield fruit. Having seen her history, she knew she was the Stella of her group—a girl child who was inquisitive, inventive and intelligent. Aunt Flossie's early support had been intentional and her "Little Quiltmaker" had developed and mastered the skills and resources to assure another generation of protection for the women in their community.

Altha hugged Aunt Flossie as the realization sank in that she was being asked to join their legacy, not as a midwife, but as one with knowledge and training from one of the premiere medical

111

institutions in America. She was a modern woman who knew the impact that tradition and community had on life. She promised to return on a regular basis, to attend quilting circles and sit at Aunt Flossie's knee and learn from Stella's journals.

As Altha stood to leave and walked past the wall of healers, she could imagine her picture up next to them.

Aunt Flossie held her hand, looked her in the eye and as if Altha was eight years old said, "My little quiltmaker."

"...ever since the first tiny bloom had opened. It had called her to come and gaze on its mystery. From barren branch stem to glistening leaf buds, from leaf bud to snowy virginity of bloom" Janie's drawing to the pear blossoms. **Zora Neal Hurston's** <u>**Their Eyes Were Watching God**</u>

CHAPTER 16

✳ ✳ ✳

LIKE THE DESERT NEEDS THE RAIN

A ltha lay in bed Sunday morning, listening to the farm wake up and watching the sun's rays lighten her window. She was thinking over her conversation with Aunt Flossie and how much she had to learn about family and community. She smiled as she fully appreciated the genius of Stella, a woman who worked with her God-given talents to help others as best she could. A renaissance woman who didn't allow her limitations to define her. She could only imagine what Stella would have accomplished in these modern times.

Altha quietly recommitted to be more and do more to help people in her life. She committed to returning home on a regular basis to be in Josiah's life and learn from Aunt Flossie. Even as she made the promise, she knew the true draw back to Dublin was Brandon T. Johnson.

She recalled how he calmly relaxed into her arms as she shared her limitless vision on life with him. How she guided him to see what she saw and helped better define his blessings and accomplishments. Somehow, she was able to avert his eyes from the painful distractions that took his focus off his beautiful daughter and her future growth. She reveled in the fact she provided for one of his needs—a new personal vision on life.

She had not expected his loving hug as a reward, but she felt as if she never wanted his nearness to end. His touch ignited a fire in her that yearned to join with him and only him. There was a newness with him and a glow of potential that she had never experienced with another man.

On this, her last day in Dublin, she would visit Tee in the morning, go to church, then afterwards, enjoy Sunday brunch at her home with Brandon, Jameli, Mrs. Baker and her mother. That night, she would head home to Atlanta and back into the shark-filled waters at work. Her heart ached to stay home in Dublin.

As she walked towards the kitchen passing the living room, Altha spied Tee's unfinished quilt. She saw the nearly four rows of cloth pieces that made a kaleidoscope of color and patterns. Now that she was able to read the quilt in a way few could, she admired the effort placed by the women.

Her focus was Aunt Flossie's starter piece that featured well placed triangles forming the underground railroads signal for the flying geese, predicting Tee should have an easy delivery. Adjusting her gaze to the top right corner of the cloth, she saw a well-tailored, red diamond. Altha blinked twice as she allowed its significance to quietly sink in. She knew that despite Tee's present strength, intelligence and professional success, due to her history, she needed the support of the quilt to assure her voice was heard by the medical system.

Four miles away, Brandon had risen early and was finishing up a morning jog. He was still trying to process what he experienced with Altha last evening. He wondered what prompted her to come wrap her arms around him then share her vision of his life with him. He recalled the warmth of her body and the rich, full tone of her voice. A voice he found to be a soothing balm for all of his worries and pain. A voice he could listen to forever. His experience during yesterday's sunset was healing and restorative. He was excited by its message for him to live.

It was the second night he had slept soundly and awakened in peace. In fact, since visiting Uncle Lou's and tasting the healing spring water, Brandon had not had any nightmares. With a good night's sleep, he found he had more energy to give his students and Jameli. He didn't know whether it was the water or the blessing he heard at the spring saying, "It is well," but he knew a pivotal change had happened in his spirit. He was energized and wanted to create. Altha's presence brought a stunning freshness to his life he thought was long past.

He would see Altha at church and then his family would join Altha and Annabelle for Sunday brunch. The day would end with Altha returning to Atlanta, and the fast-paced lifestyle she had become accustomed to. He would have to commit to some long-term plans for his life and think of what was best for Jameli. He would be actively pursuing life and putting an end to his "time out." The world was theirs for the choosing. Would they go back to Kenya, or try someplace new like London, Paris or even New York? While these were early considerations, he wished most of all there was a way to stay connected to Altha.

When Altha entered the hospital, Tee was in good spirits and was ready to be discharged home with a follow-up visit on Tuesday.

She sat on the edge of her bed. "So, I followed your advice…"

It took Tee a second to register what Altha was talking about. "Oh! Really? And?"

"It worked. Love received. Love given."

"Wow! Congrats for stepping up! Wow! You move fast, big Sis!"

"Thanks to you. Your advice was perfect. Exactly what I needed." Altha paused for a moment, thinking. "So what's Lesson Two?"

Tee laughed. But then, with sincerity in her eyes she instructed, "Try telling him the truth. No games or distractions. He's been injured by life and so will be drawn to things that are solid and dependable."

As Altha helped Tee pack to go home, she shared a short version on the origins of the quilt and how it worked, and how it had worked for Tee specifically. Tee wiped a tear, grateful that her community had rallied for her well-being. Both she and Josiah were doing well. The nurse came with a wheelchair and Altha followed her out of the hospital and helped her into James's waiting car. She promised to make Tee and James her last stop before heading back to Atlanta to give her even more details. After hugging each other, they parted.

Arriving in time for church, Altha joined her mother in the second pew. As she entered, she smiled at Brandon, Jameli and Mrs. Baker, who were sitting on the opposite side of the church a row or two back. Annabelle, during testimony time, thanked the church for their prayers of support for Tee and James.

Sitting in the church of her youth, Altha was too distracted to listen to the sermon. If her outside was controlled, underneath, her emotions were in turmoil. The only spirit she could feel was an increasing attraction to Brandon. In her Sunday best, sitting yards away from him in the air-conditioned church, her body began to sweat. Her thoughts drifted to what would have happened if she had not been called to the hospital Saturday evening.

She felt at one with Brandon when he hugged her. The natural progression was for him to kiss her and sweep her away to where they would live happily ever after. That's what should have happened yesterday and did happen in romance novels. There were many chances for him to approach her private space—at the spring, that night in front of Mrs. Baker's house, then after the game at the soccer park. He had not taken his chance and Altha realized he may not be ready.

But Altha was ready. While the preacher prayed, Altha internally hummed Alicia Key's song, "I Need You"—the song she heard first in the back seat of that red BMW in 2007. The funky-beated melody where Alicia unabashedly describes her intensity for her man's love.

I need you, Altha thought. *There will never be two things that go together better than you and me. I need you.*

Her body swayed imperceptibly as the temperature of her emotions for Brandon began to rise from deep inside her. Like a pear blossom that becomes small in the night's cool air only to expand in the day's warmth, Altha's soul began to unfold like petals positioning to receive the sun's morning rays.

Altha began tapping her foot to the tempo of her private groove as she relived being held in Brandon's powerful arms. The song called to her. *North means south, east means west and no means Yes! Yes! Yes!*

Beads of perspiration began to form on her bosom and she reached forward for a Carver Funeral Home fan and began fanning herself.

There sitting in the second row of Byrdhill Baptist Church, Altha, the introvert was lost in a heated love fantasy about Brandon T. Johnson. Her mother placed a hand on her daughter's fidgeting leg to stop Altha's toe tapping. Altha began squirming in her seat like a toddler as her body came alive with just the thoughts of being touched by Brandon again. She was taken over by the song's refrain.

Like the desert needs the rain, like joy needs pain, I need you. Hey! Hey! Hey!"

The silent buzz of her cellphone interrupted her thoughts.

She looked down and saw a text.

Brandon: Hope all is well. Are we still on for brunch?

She answered: All is well! Looking forward to brunch. Do we have unfinished business?

After an uncomfortable delay, his reply came.

Brandon: No…It's still going on. I still feel you in my arms. The nearness of you lingers on me and in me. I am rusty at the game, so I'm going back to high school. If you like me, send a thumbs up. If you see me as only friend potential, send a smiley face. But before you answer I need you to know that I'm sending you a thumbs up.

Altha wasn't expecting his reply and it tipped her emotions into a landslide as she began blushing and smiling, trying to contain her joy. Mentally riding the overwhelming drum beat of Alicia Keys' song, she thought in rhythm to the song's lines, *"Yes! Yes! Yes!"*

Altha texted back: Thumbs up x 3

After church, Annabelle and Altha met Brandon, Jameli and Mrs. Baker by the church's front door. Uncle Lou walked past, casually patting Brandon on the back while whispering, "A handsome couple."

At Annabelle's home, instead of eating indoors, they took advantage of Sonny Harkens' handmade picnic table on the side of the house that was covered by the shade of the aged, sweet gum tree. The shade and a cool breeze made it an ideal setting. As they bowed their heads, Altha held Jameli's hand in the prayer circle, giving it an extra squeeze for the Holy Ghost. The young girl smiled up at her.

The meal was chicken and waffles with sides of collard greens, peas, corn and freshly made potato pie. The conversation was lively and Jameli was the most talkative and lit up when Altha began describing the other cities she visited. Altha was taken by her and knew they would be lifelong friends.

With the meal finished, Mrs. Baker, Annabelle and Jameli cleared the table, leaving Altha and Brandon alone for the first time that day. Brandon extended his hand and asked Altha to walk with him. She slipped her hand into his, and it felt like coming home as they walked side by side.

Brandon said, "Thumbs up, hey."

Altha was quiet and gave the thumbs up sign with her hand.

Brandon asked, "What unfinished business were you texting about?"

Altha stopped walking and turned to look at him with a shy smile on her face. "Yesterday after you hugged me, you were supposed to kiss me, then we live happily ever after."

Brandon chuckled. "I know, but the phone call changed everything." With a burning desire in his eyes, he continued, "If I had the chance to do it over, I would do it differently."

Altha looked at him with inviting eyes and said, "I'll give you a do over."

As they entered the grove of blooming pear trees, Altha leaned against a tree and opened her arms, inviting him to give her a hug. Without delay, Brandon stepped into her embrace and pulled her body close to his. Altha could feel the sparks of passion between them burning bright. She felt the lightheadedness she felt in college. His breath was warm on her neck as he hugged her tight.

Before he could let go, she softly whispered in his ear, "Brandon."

"Yes," he whispered back.

She kissed his ear and said with the same unwavering intention that her Kenyan sisters had done for centuries, "I choose you."

He froze for a moment and as if those words were the magic key to open the gates of his heart. He let his emotions freely flow. He rained soft kisses onto Altha's forehead, then onto her closed eyelids then her nose, finally resting his lips gently on hers. His soft kisses rose steadily in intensity until they transitioned to powerful confident consuming tastes that weakened Altha's knees.

He held her as her body responded like the pear blooms opening to welcome the bumble bees, and an ecstatic shiver traveled down her arched spine, pulling her forward and molding her body into his.

As if all of nature and the spirit of a smiling Zora Neal Hurston were celebrating the union, white pear blossom petals began slowly falling like confetti to christen the two new young lovers.

✳ ✳ ✳

BACK IN THE WATERS

Monday morning was Altha's first day back at work. She and Brandon spoke during her drive all the way back to Atlanta and well into the night. They began the day with a prayer and the new love of Altha's life spoke with her on the way to work. He encouraged her to do her best and reassured her he had her back.

His voice was refreshing. She closed the conversation with the words she would use daily to testify her feelings for him until the coming moment when they would openly profess their love for each other.

With love she said, "Brandon, I choose you."

She could hear the smile in Brandon's voice when he answered, "Altha, I choose you."

Knowing he was on her team, no matter how new his partnership, gave her extra energy and determination. She was thankful to have him in her life and was excited for their future.

As she exited the elevator on her floor, she nearly ran into the chief of the Anesthesia Department. He curtly asked Altha to come by his office for a short, sit-down meeting at 10 am after she started her cases. Altha said she would be there, then confidently entered her office and in preparation, pulled out her file with the QA write up and her letter explaining why she had dismissed Dr. Hanson, the resident, from the room.

Today for some reason, there was no fear or back down in her. She prepared in her mind exactly what she would say to defend herself. During Mrs. Murphy's case, she said what she said as the physician leading the care team and Hanson had not listened to or processed her request. His lack of respect for her leadership was affecting her ability to provide the best care for the patient, and therefore, she asked him to leave. Simple.

Recognizing a new power that came from knowing her happiness and self-worth were anchored in Dublin, she would be free to aggressively argue her points and display her strength of character with less regard for her peers' positions.

After she started her cases, she got the file and took it into the chief's office. He directed her to a seat, saying the meeting would be short. Before she could speak, he said, "In all my years in this department, I have not received letters like these."

He held up two letters. "This one is from the ICU team and this one from the obstetrics team. The ICU chief said that the obstetrics patient you brought them last week was managed in an outstanding fashion. The obstetrics team attending wrote that you performed and supported him in a professional manner, that you were ahead in the management of the patient at each step, and that the positive outcome was in large part due to your vigilance and leadership."

He sat the letters on his desk and straightened them. He cleared his throat. "Dr. Harkens, this is exceptional. I think it's time we get behind you and push you into some leadership positions in the department. We need your type of vision and leadership to progress. Congratulations, these will be going into your permanent file."

Altha was speechless, and placed the folder meant to defend her actions with the resident back on her lap. He hadn't mentioned

Dr. Hanson so she found no reason to. That was confirmation that her actions in the crisis had been best.

After leaving the chief's office and while still processing the meeting, she ran into Dr. Manuel Romero, the junior staff with the shark, Dr. Steel, from a week ago. He approached her and said, "You know people are still talking about how well you did on that resuscitation. I really respect how you practice and want to walk through your thinking during the case so I can learn. Lunch is on me today at 12:30. I'm ready to hear your thoughts and won't take no for an answer."

Altha said, "Deal. 12:30 at the canteen," and the two colleagues shook hands.

As Altha was headed to her office, from down the hall, she heard her name called.

"Dr. Harkens, Dr. Harkens."

When she turned, she saw the towering Carlton Murphy, the husband and new father from last week. She remembered his wails and felt a sharp pain in her heart.

He hugged her and said over and over, "I know it was you. I know it was you." His voice was raspy and filled with emotion. "I was watching my daughter and saw how you kept at it, called for the surgeon to come back and were right there protecting my wife. Tasha is fine, and the baby is too. Thank you. I know it's your job and you get paid to do it, but I felt like you were looking over us. Like God was hearing my prayers and working through you."

Altha was speechless for a moment. Then she smiled and told him, "You're welcome. It was my honor to fight for her life and for your family. I'm thankful to God for the great outcome. Please tell your wife I said hello."

Before he could get out of earshot, she asked, "What did you end up naming the baby?"

He smiled broadly, "Marie Altha Murphy. Thanks, Doc."

Tears welled up in Altha's eyes. They hugged one more time and then she turned to go to her office before the tears threatened to fall. She smiled as she closed her office door behind her. Some days are good, but this day was shaping up to be great. In the privacy of her office, she graciously fell to her knees in prayer giving thanks for her new blessings. She was thankful for her Dublin community, her caring mother, her wise sister, her beautiful nephew, her new love and her coming legacy as a new Quiltmaker.

The End

Wisdom's Afterword

✳ ✳ ✳

In the U.S., Black women die at three times the rate of their white sisters surrounding childbirth. Georgia has the highest death rate for women during childbirth in the nation. The causes are still unclear, but range from poor access to health care, access but not being heard by the medical establishment, avoidance of touch due to prior trauma, and mistrust of the healthcare system due to prior personal or related adverse events. The new "Hear Her" campaign by the Centers For Disease Control is a great place to learn more (www.cdc.gov/hearher).

These are some measures that can be taken today by mothers and their support teams that will move the needle in a positive direction.

A. **A WOMAN IS PREGNANT 45 WEEKS! 39 Weeks With Child and 6 Weeks Without.**
   You are considered pregnant from the time you get pregnant until six weeks after you deliver. Up until six weeks after you deliver, your body may have complications from the birth that could be life threatening. 60% of all deaths surrounding childbirth occur after the child has been delivered.

B. **SPEAK OUT OR SHOUT OUT**. If you are pregnant and have a problem, you must "Speak Out and Shout Out" to make sure your voice and needs are heard. If you present to an urgent care center or emergency room while in the forty-five-week time you are pregnant or recently delivered, insist that an obstetrician see you before you are discharged. Don't assume the system is attuned to your voice. You may have to repeat your needs multiple ways and get hospital patient advocacy involved early in order to make sure your voice is being heard and your health is being protected.

C. **EIGHT IS EXCELLENT.** There are eight times you must be seen by your obstetrician before you deliver so potential problems can be identified early.

1. When you get pregnant, they do initial labs.
2. An ultrasound to get an accurate date.
3. Genetic testing.
4. Growth check and ultrasound to make sure the body parts are growing right.
5. When the placenta is large enough to cause problems like high blood pressure, your weight and urine will be checked each visit. Rapid weight gain and protein in the urine may mean early preeclampsia.
6. Checks to make sure the blood pressure, sugar, weight gain and urine protein are good.
7. Checks to make sure the blood pressure, sugar, weight gain and urine protein are good.
8. To make sure the baby is turned right and lined up right with the birthing canal.

D. BLACK WOMEN AND SEXUAL ASSAULT

1. One in four Black girls will be sexually abused before age eighteen.

2. 40 to 60% of Black women report being subjected to coercive sexual contact by age eighteen.
3. One in five Black women are survivors of rape.
4. For every Black woman who reports a rape, fifteen do not.

The Cause

✳ ✳ ✳

Partial Proceeds will go to support
The Black Mamas Matter Alliance
1237 Ralph David Abernathy Blvd
Atlanta GA 30310
info@blackmamasmatter.org
Donation Link https://www.mightycause.com/organization/
Black-Mamas-Matter-Alliance

Acknowledgements

∗ ∗ ∗

Special thanks to my partner for the story, Ms. Cassandra Edmond, my sister, true friend and the first renaissance woman I ever knew. One whose love sees the full playing field of life as she stands as a silent, wise protector of her family and its future. Blessings and praise in honor of both sides of the family, those Red Eyed Edmonds and the family Saints who constantly battle to move the generations forward in their own way. Gone but not forgotten, and prayerfully and respectfully to the memories of our Uncle Jacob" Sonny," Edmond, Uncle J.T. Edmond, Uncle Lou Edmond and Uncle "Buddy" Edmond. In respectful memory of their mother Magnolia Edmond.

In honor of Estella Pryor and her prodigy; special thanks to Mr. Robert Pryor, Estella's 100-year-old son, and her granddaughter, Mrs. Barbara Pryor George, who cared enough to share. In memory of Aunt Annabelle Wilson, and Aunt Flossie. With love to Mrs. Anne Jordan, Mrs. Evelyn Weaver and Miss Joyce McKay. Thanks to Mrs. Eudell Sleighmon, Tory English, Barbara Edmond, sisters Joy and Rachel Barnes, Victoria Ladelle CRNA, Attorney Kathleen Edmond, Dr. Keisha Nieto. Special thanks to Dr. Dazon Dixon Diallo of Sister Love Inc -Women's Advocacy. With praise for BirdHill Baptist Church Dudley, Georgia.

Professional thanks to the current group of obstetricians who are diligently studying the issue of Black mothers' mortality and daily fighting the battle to provide quality care to their patients. To the midwives of the 20th century who at one time delivered upwards of 75% of rural babies, and to current midwives knowing their efforts are still recognized.

To the artisans and quiltmakers among us especially Mr. Rudd Van Empel and Mr. Orlando The Designer

To the Beta Readers, Mrs. Deborah Bolden, Mrs. April McCoy RN, Dr. Angela Perry, Dr. Tim Brown, Dr. Mary Lindsay, Mrs. Lee Dorothy Edmond, and Dr. Cheryl Sawyers. Dr. Candice Jones-Cox, Dr. Lisbeth Pappas, Mrs Janet Rono- Kenyan Advisor
Special Editors: Ms. Lillian Adu, Ms. Kathy Stanley, Dr. Sherri Lewis
To The DreamHouse Marketing Team of Ms. Zsa Zsa Lambert Hall and Mrs. Candis White

References

* * *

STORY SUBJECTS

To find out more about the story visit www.bedmondproject.com
Alicia Keys' song, "I Need You
    https://www.youtube.com/watch?v=B8vJNcBy4Pc
The art of Ruud Van Empel can be found at: www.ruudvanempel.nl
    and www.jacksonfineart.com. The latter is where my work is
    for sale in Atlanta.
"How to Swim With Sharks: A Primer" by Voltaire Cousteau Dinner
    Talk by Richard Johns circa 1974 *Trans Assoc Am Physicians*
    1975:88:44-54

DEATH OF BLACK WOMEN DURING PREGNANCY

Georgia Birth Advocacy Coalition Link https://georgiabirth.org/
"America is Failing Its Black Mothers" Harvard Public Health
    https://www.hsph.harvard.edu/magazine/magazine_article/
    america-is-failing-its-black-mothers/
"Why Americas Black Mothers and Babies are in a Life or Death
    Crisis " *New York Times* Apr 11, 2018
    https://www.nytimes.com/2018/04/11/magazine/black-
    mothers-babies-death-maternal-mortality.html

"Understanding Maternal Mortality Rates Among Black Women"
June 13, 2021
https://www.stkate.edu/academics/healthcare-degrees/
black-women-maternal-mortalit Black Midwives
Racial Ethnic Disparities in Pregnancy Related Deaths – United
States 2007-2016 by E. Peterson, Weekly/September6,2019
68(35) ; 762-765,
https://www.cdc.gov/mmwr/volumes/68/wr/mm6835a3.htm

BLACK MIDWIVES

Black midwifery in the United States: Past, present, and future
https://onlinelibrary.wiley.com › doi › soc4
https://onlinelibrary.wiley.com/doi/10.1111/soc4.12829
TBT : Granny Midwives of the South May 19, 2015
https://www.colorlines.com/articles/tbt-granny-midwives-south

BLACK WOMEN AND SEXUAL VIOLENCE

"Black women the forgotten survivors of sexual assault: African
American women are at disproportionate risk of sexual
violence. Here's how you can help." American Psychological
Association , In the Public Interest Feb 2020
By Jameta Nicole Barlow PhD MPH
National Center on Violence Against Women in the Black
Community
https://ujimacommunity.org/wpcontent/uploads/2018/12Ujima-
Womens-Violence-Stats-v7.4-.1pdf

About The Authors

✳ ✳ ✳

The authors are both offspring of Holman Edmond and Lee Dorothy Edmond. The siblings are the best of friends and confidants. They shared the support from their siblings, Lori Lee Paschal and Dr. Rod Edmond.

Miss Cassandra Edmond is a product of Southwest Atlanta and has been active in community services for decades. She is an avid reader, art enthusiast, and cultural historian. Over the years, she has mentored, coached, and supported countless young women along their paths to success. She is a renaissance woman in the truest sense. This is her first foray into the field of storytelling through the written word. Her message for the world is to be hopeful and ever mindful that, "No weapon for against you shall prosper."

Dr. B.K. Edmond is a medical doctor, husband, father, brother, son and friend. Raised in southwest Atlanta and a product of an HBCU and Ivy League higher education, he is constantly seeking new ways to serve. He has seen healthcare from the provider side, the patient side and as a member of the patient support team. This is his third use of the written medium to expand his service commitment. His daily prayer is to have a crystal-clear mind so as to use the full scope of his knowledge to effectively care for his patients; to have a silver tongue so that he might communicate in a seamless manner with the care team; and to have a heart of gold such that no man may have cause to question his honorable intentions.

Visit www.TheBEdmondProject.com